Also by Walter Wangerin Jr.

The Book of God:
The Bible as a Novel

Paul: A Novel

Jesus: A Novel

Letters from the Land
of Cancer

This Earthly Pilgrimage

Saint Julian

The Book of the Dun Cow

The Book of Sorrows

Preparing for Jesus

Reliving the Passion

Little Lamb, Who Made Thee?

The Manger Is Empty

Miz Lil and the Chronicles
of Grace

Mourning into Dancing

The Orphean Passages

Ragman and Other Cries
of Faith

Whole Prayer

In the Days of the Angels

As For Me and My House

The Crying for a Vision

For Children

Mary's First Christmas

Peter's First Easter

The Book of God for Children

Probity Jones and The Fear-Not Angel

Thistle

Potter

In the Beginning There Was No Sky

Angels and All Children

Water, Come Down

The Bedtime Rhyme

Swallowing the Golden Stone

Branta and the Golden Stone

Elisabeth and the Water Troll

NAOMI
AND HER
DAUGHTERS

NAOMI
AND HER
DAUGHTERS

A NOVEL

by WALTER
WANGERIN JR
NATIONAL BOOK AWARD WINNING AUTHOR

ZONDERVAN.com/
AUTHORTRACKER
follow your favorite authors

We want to hear from you. Please send your comments about this book to us in care of zreview@zondervan.com. Thank you.

ZONDERVAN

Naomi and Her Daughters
Copyright © 2010 by Walter Wangerin, Jr. and/or Ruthanne M. Wangerin as Trustee of Trust No. 1.

This title is also available as a Zondervan ebook.
Visit www.zondervan.com/ebooks.

This title is also available in a Zondervan audio edition.
Visit www.zondervan.fm.

Requests for information should be addressed to:

Zondervan, *Grand Rapids, Michigan 49530*

Library of Congress Cataloging-in-Publication Data

Wangerin, Walter.
    Naomi and her daughters : a novel / Walter Wangerin, Jr.
      p. cm.
    ISBN 978-0-310-32734-9 (hardcover, jacketed)
    1. Naomi (Biblical figure) — Fiction. 2. Mothers and daughters — Fiction. 3. Bible.
    O.T. — History of Biblical events — Fiction. 4. Women in the Bible — Fiction. I. Title.
    PS3573.A477   N36 2010
    813'.54 — dc22   2010019078

Published in association with the Anderson Literary Agency.

Cover and interior illustration: © 2010 by Joel Spector
Interior design: Beth Shagene, Christine Orejuela-Winkelman
Editorial team: Bob Hudson, Amy Allen, Elaine Schnabel

Printed in the United States of America

10 11 12 13 14 15 /DCI/ 23 22 21 20 19 18 17 16 15 14 13 12 11 10 9 8 7 6 5 4 3 2 1

For Paul Danger,
My Faithful Aaron

NAOMI
AND HER
DAUGHTERS

Part One

MILCAH

1

A Present Rage

A cry is heard in Judah, lamentation and bitter weeping. The Women of Bethlehem are weeping for their daughter and refusing to be consoled because she is no more.

Four hundred women in black robes stand on rooftops. They tear their hair. They stretch their arms wide under heaven. They throw back their heads and whirl, robes billowing.

"Milcah!" they howl, wolves keening on the air. "Milcah!"

Milcah of the white hands, sixteen years old, the young wife whose cheeks they kissed not three days ago and unto whom they waved farewell as she departed with her husband for his home in Ephraim—Milcah is no more.

She will never come home again.

Until the evening meal this had been an unremarkable day. By midafternoon the women were preparing for supper by grinding grain in their handmills—producing the genial sound of a village at work. Children small enough still to be playing in the lanes began to smell barley cakes baking. Time to twaddle home. As the sun descended and shadows grew too long for labor, the farmers came back through the gate. They paused in the public square to discuss the date harvest—difficult because the palms grew far down great escarpments near the shores of the Salt Sea.

Just before they separated, while each farmer turned to his house, a man came sprinting into town. He fell to his knees and gasped for air.

He wore a loincloth only. He had the long, ropy muscles of a distance runner. He carried the leather envelope of a messenger. It went spinning across the ground with the force of his fall. His hair was stuck to his forehead with sweat.

The farmers formed a ring around the man.

One of them shouted toward a near house: "Miriam! Bring water!"

The urgency of his voice and the hubbub in the square drew wives and mothers out of doors. The small children jumped up on bench-backs in order to see. It isn't often that events break the easy routines of Bethlehem.

"A full skin of water!" The farmer squatted beside the messenger. "Take your time," he said. He helped the breathless fellow to a stone bench, then sat down beside him.

Miriam arrived. "Salmon," she said and handed a goat's bladder to her husband. Peering around the woman's skirts was a wide-eyed little girl, winding long hair around a forefinger. "Papa?"

Salmon tipped the messenger's head back and squirted

a stream of water into his mouth. The poor fellow's eyes were red with September dust and salt sweat. Salmon poured water over the messenger's head, moistened the edge of his own tunic and washed the runner's eyes.

"Can you speak?"

The runner nodded, then croaked, "Yes." He paused a moment, then said, "A Levite …"

"Take your time."

"A Levite …"

At the same time a tall man bent down, picked up the messenger's leather envelope and began to open its flap.

The messenger yelled, "No! Don't do that!"

Salmon looked up. "Boaz," he snapped. *Stop!"*

Boaz showed no intention of stopping. He opened the envelope altogether. Everyone was watching him now. He glanced in. He shuddered and tipped the bag over and out fell a human hand.

Immediately Miriam grabbed her child and hurried away.

Men grew solemn; some of the women covered their mouths. Some stepped closer, disbelieving.

Yes. *(Oh, Lord God!)* It was a human hand chopped clean off above the wrist, its skin as white and as dry as ivory. The hand was loosely fisted. Two bones showed in the chop, the marrows shrunk into pits.

"Put it down," Salmon commanded. "Put it down!"

Boaz had regained his insouciance. "Shouldn't we burn it?" he grinned. "As an offering?"

The messenger raised his voice. "A Levite from Ephraim sent me to Judah and especially—" He stopped and swallowed. "Especially to Bethlehem," he said, and more softly, "to you. One of your daughters has perished."

A perfect silence fell on the village. Even the children who could not understand his words began to suffer their parents' distress.

He stood up, then took a stand on the bench. "I'm one of twelve who have been commanded to inform every tribe in Israel. This Levite, his wife—" the messenger grew stiff and emotionless. "The Levite's wife, whom you know as Milcah, was raped by the men of Gibeah. She is dead."

If dogs were skulking about the village square or goats running loose; if birds were fluttering in the dust, no one was aware of it. The sun sat down on its western ridge and reddened with regret.

So the Women of Bethlehem turned away and left the men behind them in the village square. They pulled the scarves from their heads and let the cloth fall in heaps. Older women bared their breasts and began to beat them in a slow rhythm. Others donned black, climbed the stairs to the roofs of their houses, and lifted their voices in lamentation. *Rachel, weeping for her children.*

WHILE THEY WAIL ABOVE, one woman remains below. She has set her jaw, her chin thrust forward, her countenance hard-eyed and rigid. When she begins to move, the men make way for her. She kneels down. Tenderly she wraps Milcah's hand in her scarf. She rises and walks to the gate, to stone steps that take her to the watchman's room above.

Iron-eyed, she looks through the northern window. The

wind begins to whirl her hair. She holds Milcah's hand, now respectfully clothed for burial, in both of hers and stretches it forth toward Gibeah. "Be not silent," she begins to sing in a level, deliberate rage:

> *Be not silent, God of my praise;*
> *for the wicked and the deceitful*
> *have assaulted her without cause.*
> *They reward her goodness with evil*
> *and her love with hatred.*

The rest of the Women of Bethlehem hear a canticle of anger.

Naomi, they think, and they mute their miseries. For this is she. This is Bethlehem's Hakamah, whose song gives language to their bitterness.

> *Let their days be few—*
> *Let others seize their goods—*
> *Let their daughters be fatherless,*
> *their wives made widows!*
> *Let their sons be driven*
> *from a city destroyed*
> *into the countryside to tap with sticks*
> *the rims of beggars' bowls!*

Naomi has lived thirty-five years on these upland hills. Sun and the unrelenting summers have scored her face with a thousand wrinkles. In repose her face is wreathed with the vines of kindness. But at this moment it is as severe and cracked as dry clay. Northward, even to Gibeah nine miles hence, the watchwoman of Bethlehem cries her curses:

Let no one—no one!—be kind to the
   wives of the wicked
    or pity their fatherless children.
Cut them off from the earth, O Lord!
   Blot out their names by the second generation—
For they did not remember mercy.
   They took the gentle Milcah
   and broke her soul to death.

The sun has concealed itself behind the farther ridge, spreading a fire of shame across the pillars of heaven. The hilltops grow ashen.

Naomi is a Mother in Israel, a Hakamah, the teller of the tales of Israel's past. She sings songs that name her people's bewilderment, songs to give order to the wild complexities of their existence, songs to collect their mute emotions into a spear of cursings or the milk of blessing.

Mine is an outcry against Gibeah. Come, O Lord, and judge the truth of my outcry. Send your angels. Send angels to destroy the wicked city.

Long into the darkness Naomi keeps watch over Bethlehem. Finally, at midnight, she descends the stone steps and departs through the village gate and walks by memory the road to Rachel's tomb a mile northward. There she scoops out a dusty hole. Into its bed she places Milcah's hand, and prays.

But this is only one piece of her daughter. There are eleven more scattered throughout Israel, and who will love her well enough to bury those? What man could sever the corpse of his wife, even if for signs to alert the tribes of Israel?

Has such a thing ever happened in this land, since the days we came out of Egypt?

By his messengers the Levite cries out: *Behold, people of Israel, all of you, give your advice and counsel here.*

Which is to say: "To your tents, O Israel!"

2

A Motherless Child

IN TIMES OF CONTENTMENT, THE WOMEN OF BETHLEHEM gather at daybreak, each with a large jar on her head, then troop out of the village to the cistern. There is neither a spring nor a well upon these Judean hills—hence the great cistern dug and well-plastered in the mouth of a cave. Morning gossip is as nourishing as bread for untroubled maids and mothers, those who sustain and stabilize their households.

When she was twenty-two—having lived six years the wife of Elimelech—Naomi joined in that laughing camaraderie as cheerfully as anyone else. But there were differences. When she trained as a healer in Judah, the differences became apparent. As friendly as her sisters were, they felt a kind of awe. Medicines were becoming Naomi's province. She grew wise in the ways of herbs and poultices, the binding of broken bones, midwifery, philters. Healing required knowledge of incantations, formulas by which to call upon the Lord who declares: *I, even I, am he, and there*

*is no god beside me. I kill and I make alive. I wound and I
heal.*

Something like a priestess was Naomi. One who stands
between the chosen people and the deity who chose them,
comforting the one and calling upon the other.

Women of Bethlehem, the old and the young, honored
their Hakamah. They took her for a woman like themselves, of course: wife and mother and a singer when they
danced. At the same time they granted her a central place
in their lives: the keeper of their histories, the fire of their
imaginations. And they granted her solitude.

So Naomi drew her water last and alone.

These days she would sit in the semi-darkness on interior stones, abolishing thought, resting her hands on her
belly. This took the place of thinking: that now and again
her baby moved, filling all the hollows inside of her.

"Mama—"

What was that? Naomi, what did you hear?

"Mamaaaa." A small sadness farther back in the cave.
A child.

Naomi stood. She dipped a ladle into the jar she had
already filled, and began to feel her way away from daylight into gloom.

She said, "Nevermind me. Sometimes I carry cool
drinks in case somebody somewhere gets thirsty."

Immediately Naomi could hear a mighty effort at
silence. She blinked, adjusting her eyes to the dimness.
Why, there. In a small crevice a child crouched, her pale
kneecaps giving her away. Naomi, barefoot, made scarcely
a sound. So she talked.

"Well, look at this. A little girl." She paused and hummed a little tune. See? All things are right in the world. Naomi said, "Little girl, are you sad?"

The eyes were shadows till the girl lifted her face. She looked at Naomi and a fresh sob flared the child's nose.

"Yes, yes. The child is sad," said Naomi. "Can I sit down beside her? Do you think she would allow me?"

The child did not say *No*.

As she sat, the woman said, "I wonder what's my daughter's name. Would she like a drink? Crying always makes me thirsty." The child was filthy. Her flesh gave forth a foul odor.

Naomi lifted the ladle to the girl who slurped and swallowed.

"Taste good?"

The child nodded.

"What's your name?"

Like the peeping of a sparrow: "Milcah."

"Good morning, Milcah. I'm glad to meet you." Naomi sat and gazed forward, offering companionship and asking nothing in return. Then she noticed a large water jar behind the little Milcah. "Your mother couldn't come to the cistern this morning?"

The child shook her head, then covered her face and the great rain of sorrow poured down. Naomi put her arm around thin shoulders, bones as crackable as twigs.

When the tears subsided, Naomi tested a delicate matter: "Please, Milcah. I'm right here beside you. Who is your mother?"

It was as if Naomi had said, *What* is your mother. The child answered, "Dead."

"Oh, daughter, I am so sorry! Does anyone know this? Who is your father?"

The girl pressed into the woman. She whispered, "Ezra."

Ah, then here was the reason why the girl smelled as if she wore something rotten around her neck. Ezra was the tanner for the village. Tanning creates a putrid odor.

"Ezra the tanner?" Naomi said.

Uttering his name may have released the detail for which Naomi had not asked: "Mama died yesterday. Papa buried her under the floor."

THE TANNER'S HOUSE WAS NO MORE than a two-room hovel, the roof-clay cracked, straw and brambles hanging loose through the cross-branches.

Of course a woman would die in here.

Through the doorway Naomi saw walls unplastered, damp, mold blacking the corners, rats scratching the roof beams.

Though water was precious in the hill country, Naomi had washed the girl before bringing her to her Ezra—and was moved to find beneath the filth a skin almost luminous. She had anointed Milcah top to toe with scented olive oil, but the odor of animal rot and boiled oak-galls remained.

Ezra was sitting on a stool in front of his doorway. He didn't turn when the woman and the child had approached. He kept scraping flesh from a hide stretched taut over a wooden frame. He slung fat from the edge of his scraper onto a fly-blown pile between his feet.

"So," he growled. "You washed her. Does the mighty Hakamah expect thanks from a tanner's wretched mouth?"

"No, sir. I don't expect civility." The rancid atmosphere disgusted Naomi. She set down Milcah's large jar of water.

All her life the woman had been and would be direct. She said, "If you're willing, Tanner, I will take care of your daughter. I'll keep her as my own child."

Scraping, scraping. The knuckles on both his forefingers were knobbed. A touch of arthritis. He froze a moment, neither dropping his arms nor looking up.

Milcah stole to her father's side. She laid her cheek on his back and began to pat his bare ribs. The man didn't speak.

Naomi said, "I'm sorry we didn't know your wife was so ill. I promise, I would have come to sit by her pallet, Ezra. I would have prepared her body for burial—if we had known."

"Pity, pity, coming around with a hang-dog face. Suddenly the Tanner's worth the notice." He threw himself back into his work. "Brings him water who never brought him nothing before. Wants to take his child away from him."

"No. Not *away*. I'll watch her during the day—" Milcah began to mew, rubbing her cheek against her father's spine. "I'll bring you both bread as long as you both are in mourning. I'll wash her, I'll oil—"

"Get outa here," he growled.

Milcah, in her fluted voice, repeated it: "Get outa here."

Milcah, what's happened to you? Naomi's stomach knotted.

She said, "Be reasonable. Who's to care for your daughter, now that her mother's gone?"

Now Ezra turned and pointed his curved scraping knife at Naomi. Favoring the grossly knuckled fingers. Arthritis. "Who's to watch out for *me*," he growled, "now my wife's gone? You tell me that! Who takes care of the widower? My daughter, is who. All I got's my little girl." A whining crept into his voice. "My child to grind our handful of barley grain. Stick a thumb-sized spot of dough to the side of the fire pot. Clip my toenails. Bereave me! Bereave me of all what's mine! Blot out my family?"

Little Milcah had started to cry again. "Papa, don't be sad. I don't want you sad."

NAOMI WOULD HAVE SENT ELIMELECH to the Tanner. Ezra cowered in the presence of her husband.

But other matters intervened.

In two weeks Naomi went into labor. She survived the danger, as did her son. Naomi brought to her husband a second son whom she named Chilion, a baby to his brother Mahlon, who was already four years old.

3

Military Preparations

TO YOUR TENTS, O ISRAEL!

The men of Bethlehem respond immediately to the Levite's challenge. They do not sleep. All night long they prepare to march north to Mizpah, where all the tribes will mass their armies to punish the perversions of Gibeah.

Twelve tribes have been called out against the men of one city. But Gibeah is of the tribe of Benjamin, and Benjamin chooses to defend its men, however horrible the rest may judge their crime.

"Rapists!" cries Israel.

"We will see to our own," Benjamin answers.

In torchlight the men of Bethlehem sharpen their daggers, their curved swords, the heads of their spears on small whetstones. They oil the leather of their shields, gather maces, clubs and battle-axes for hand-to-hand combat, pull on the boots their wives have sewn especially for warfare.

Torch-fires play across the men's arms, slick with sweat. Salmon and Elimelech labor outside the city, equipping a four-wheeled supply wagon. They set slat-wood panels on all four sides and grease the oaken axles with animal fat. No need to speak. The two men have been friends since their boyhood—both of them Ephrathites. Each knows the other, heart and soul.

So they rub supple the stiffened leather reins and as wheelwrights repair splintered spokes.

Elimelech's sons are fifteen and eleven. Mahlon's old enough to follow his father into war. Chilion is too young. There's no help for it but that he stay home and see to the harvests. Despite the separation to come, the brothers work silently in the courtyard of their father's house: trimming and waxing reed shafts; driving the tangs of flint arrowheads into the split ends of the shafts and binding them with leather thongs soaked in water. When the thongs dry, the knots will shrink into a hold as hard as bone.

Salmon has one son, Boaz, twenty years old, and the little girl that hides behind her mother's skirts. Miriam calls her "My Balm." He calls her, "Basemath."

Boaz would rather work alone. He is restoring a mail shirt to battle readiness: sewing fresh bronze scales into the gaps torn open by previous battles. Because he is six inches taller than his father, Boaz will add several rows of scales around the bottom of the linen. He has already rewoven tough cord around the outside brim of a rawhide helmet, and has lined the inside with the thickness of felt which will fit his own head comfortably.

For her part, Naomi busies herself with food. She refuses to look at her sons where they work—though theirs is the only lamp in the courtyard. Mahlon is weeping. Soundlessly. She knows his grief by the interruptions of his breath.

From a ceiling beam Naomi unties strings of newly dried figs. She sits and slaps the figs into loaves. She'll tuck cheese in their packs, and barley cakes as hard as walnuts, and parched grain, and two skins of wine.

In the wee hours of the morning Elimelech walks straight through the courtyard and into his house and into the storeroom. He reaches to a high shelf and takes down a triangular boxwood case. He opens the case and removes his own most precious weapon: the composite bow he built against occasions like this. Strong on the draw, it shoots with an astonishing accuracy some hundred and ten paces farther than the best wooden bow. But constructed of three layers glued together—horn and wood and sinew— the weapon is vulnerable to a sideways blow. Hence the case in which he will carry the bow quick-march, even to the face of the enemy.

We are here, Naomi thinks. *Right now, in this pure moment, we are all still at home.*

DAWN SHOWS GREY ABOVE THE EASTERN HILLS—a black horizon shirred by lines of standing trees. Stars fade over the Great Salt Sea, though they still prick the darker western sky.

Families have gathered along the narrow road outside the gate, murmuring farewells and courage, uttering psalms to the Lord.

A train of wagons has been lined up in front of the congregation of Bethlehem. The oxen stand waiting in their shafts. Goatskin tents and rope, tools, stakes, weapons, bandages, foodstuffs and all the necessary supplies fill the wagons. Youths will goad the strong beasts forward, Mahlon among them, while Elimelech will share the lead with Salmon and the several other chiefs.

Naomi approaches her eldest son. She slips a packet of raisins and another of dates into his scrip.

"I am not going to cry for you," she whispers. "But I will consider you dead until I hear the news that you are alive. Better good news at the end than news that must kill me too. I refuse tears. I will stare dry-eyed at God and cry, 'Who chooses to send the sons of Israel's mothers into the dusts of death?'"

Suddenly Naomi slaps her firstborn hard in his face and walks away.

At Elimelech's side she whispers, "We're the ones who raised her dowry. We persuaded Milcah to marry the Levite."

"The truth, Naomi," her husband says without judgment. "You were the one. You persuaded her."

After a moment: "I confess it."

The man and the woman are shadows, each to the other. Even if they tried, they couldn't interpret their facial expressions. Naomi suffers a mortal weight.

"And told her ... is it only four days ago, Elimelech? When she had fled the man, I told her to go back home with him. Four days."

"Naomi." Elimelech is a man who touches his wife

without shame. He says, "If there is fault, the fault belongs to Gibeah."

Naomi murmurs: "Rain brimstone on the wicked city, O Lord almighty God."

A LITTLE CHILD SLIPS AWAY from her parents, the one her mother calls, "My Balm." She says, "Anyone seen Boaz? Someone know where my brother is?"

When she finds him she takes hold of his hand. "Bozy? Boaz?"

"What."

"You gotta promise me?" The child is fiercely intent.

"*What*, Basemath? You don't belong out here. Promise you *what?*"

"To come back."

"You don't know anything about war."

Basemath wipes tears on the back of her brother's hand. He pulls it away.

"Hush up, girl!"

She persists. She takes hold of his short tunic and yanks it. "You *got* to promise! I won't let go till you promise."

"Oh, all right."

"No, Boaz. Say it out loud."

"Say what?"

"To come back home again."

"Basemath! Child!" This is Salmon sounding anxious. "Where are you?"

Boaz says, "I promise. Yes. I will come back home again."

His sister wipes her face in his tunic, then grabs his hand again and holds it up. "Here we are, Papa!"

Salmon swims through the people in their direction. "Don't do that to us," he scolds as he comes near. "Your mother's gone back to the city looking for you. Time's running out. Let's go find her."

But first he scrutinizes his son. "Boaz? Are you okay? Surely unafraid. Stouthearted?"

"Why wouldn't I be?"

"Well, forgive me. It's the old tenderness of a father. Or an old father's tenderness."

He swings his daughter onto his shoulders. "You be my lookout." He starts, then glances back to Boaz. "Have you seen my mail shirt? My helmet? I couldn't find them last night."

WHEN THE SOLDIERS ARRIVE AT MIZPAH TONIGHT, chiefs of every tribe will set up an altar and offer sacrifices. Because of his sacred office, the Levite will be expected to inquire of the Lord their God: *How shall we proceed against the Benjamites?*

As for now, this moment, the dews exhale a morning mist. Mist fills the valleys as whey fills clay bowls. The armies march in a ragged line, descending into whiteness and are gone.

Suddenly sunrise shoots a bloody radiance through the low fog, while the women stand and watch.

Guard their lives, O Lord. Do not let them be put to shame.

4

Mahlon and Milcah
Sit Down to Play

IN THE SPRING OF LITTLE MILCAH'S FIFTH YEAR (according to Naomi's calculations) the child contracted an oozing infection in both her eyes. The eyelashes crusted. Even the whites of her eyeballs were shot through with a painful redness.

As she had before, Naomi still lingered alone in the mouth of the cave, watching. Day after day Milcah showed up with her jar and stood with her eyes fixed on the ground, saying nothing while Naomi lifted the heavy cover from the neck of the cistern.

Neither did Naomi talk. She bided her time, hoping to earn the child's trust by repeating this single act of kindness, requiring nothing of Milcah in return.

When she felt the time right, Naomi brought cakes and fruit and milk, leaving them beside the cistern, saying nothing. The child looked but hesitated to touch the food for several days. Finally hunger persuaded her to snatch what she could hold with a jar on her head, and carry them both home.

In time the woman and the girl sat and ate bread together.

It took serious restraint not to say *something* to Milcah. Bruises proved that her father beat her. Even under the unwashed filth, welts rose up on the backs of her thighs. Her hair was impossible. In sunlight Naomi saw lice jumping.

Several times she encountered Ezra and Milcah in the city. As soon as the child caught sight of Naomi, she seized her father's hand and kissed it, murmuring, "Love you, Papa, love you, love you," refusing to admit the older woman's presence.

And then that eye infection.

In the mornings Milcah was rubbing the itchings with the knuckles of both hands, which only inflamed the eyes and swelled the lids to slits. The girl was crippled. Soon she emerged before the other women since her eyes were burned blind by the hard morning's sun.

Naomi suffered a day of panic, but on the second day found Milcah's jar empty inside the cave. No, no, the child hadn't the strength to lift the lid. Oh, what a thrashing she must have received at home.

Papa needs me. Papa needs me.

But one need produces another need. In order to feed and water her father, Milcah needed to be whole. In order to approximate wholeness, she accepted Naomi's medicines without protesting.

Before dawn the following day, Naomi arrived just as Milcah did. She ran the pad of her forefinger over a thick syrup in a stone pot. The salve had been prepared from the seeds of the fennel plant.

The coolness kept the child sitting still. Naomi spoke in a soft, motherly voice. "Please. Let me spread my lotion on your eyes for four or five days, and you will see again."

Naomi removed the heavy cistern lid, filled the girl's jar, and helped her balance the tall clay on her head.

Sight established a delicate relationship.

Milcah began to accept small amounts of wheat flour and salt. At home she baked the bread herself. Her father never noticed the giftiness of his food. Or if he did, he didn't dispute it.

Naomi taught Milcah weaving on her own loom. She taught the child simple sewing: the whipstitch of a beginner.

ALREADY AFTER HIS THIRD BIRTHDAY Chilion took delight in the sheer motion of his body. He ran races with boys who were one and two years older than he—and though he mostly lost, he never came in last, nor was disappointed in his performance. Chilion was convinced that the day would come when he would outrun every boy in the village—except Mahlon, of course.

Elimelech laughed to see such determination in his son's face. Moreover, watching the windblown loops of Chilion's dark brown hair put him in mind of the freedoms he had known as a child. Elimelech made a small bow for his son and several blunted arrows, and taught him how to shoot rats and hares and a mouse at full skitter.

Mahlon, on the other hand, tended toward the contemplative life. While his brother grew restive during the rainy seasons, Mahlon appreciated the chance to linger dry inside his house. He listened to the tales his mother spun while she sat working at her loom.

Pharaoh, slopping through stinking heaps of rotting frogs. Gnats beclouding the Egyptian air, gnats clustered on Pharaoh's eyelids and his nostrils, sipping little drinks.

Naomi paused and said to her son: "The Lord our God made a covenant with us at Sinai. Not with our ancestors did the Lord make this covenant, but with us, Mahlon, you and me and our family and Bethlehem and Israel, all of us who are alive today. He spoke with *us* face-to-face at the mountain, out of the midst of the fire.

"Now then, listen to me. Memorize this commandment word for word. In time teach it to your children when you sit in your own house:

"*Hear, O Israel: the Lord our God is one Lord. And you shall love the Lord your God with all your heart, and with all your soul, and with all your might!*"

Mahlon memorized the commandment. He repeated the stories Naomi told. Obedience came easily, and love for the Lord consumed him.

In contrast to his brother, Mahlon took his pleasure in the motions of his mind, which he exercised by playing board games—inside, under the pounding rain, outside under the pounding sun. He tossed knucklebones, moved pieces over the twenty squares he had etched into a limestone board, training himself in visual geometries, mathematics, strategies, foresight, mental planning and a modest triumph.

This was the kind of contest his father might admire but hadn't the patience to play. Nor were his mother's hands free in the daylight. After sunset she was often called to other houses, chanting incantations, administering medicines.

The only person happy to play a game with him was Milcah. Even at six, one year younger than Mahlon, the little maiden was capable of surprising moves and, now and then, gleefully, of victory. Mahlon never let her win. It wasn't necessary. The child accepted the truth of things without complaint. Besides, both of them knew that she was improving.

Naomi thought: *The child who lives in the midst of abuse lives a life of losses.*

The timorous Milcah had begun to test boldness.

Naomi still maintained a certain formality between herself and the child. Generous with food and a tender countenance and with pieces of fresh clothing, yet she would not permit herself to probe into Milcah's home life. Oh, but how full the woman was with gratitude, for the Lord had encouraged friendship between her son and the girl. Simple games gave them both contentment.

Too much contentment, sometimes. The time passes faster than they realize.

So it was that in the middle of one afternoon Milcah was shocked to hear the clapping of two flat boards together: *Crack! Crack!*

Terrified, she leaped to her feet and flew from the house and into the rain without a word.

Crack!

Her father had discovered her absence. Naomi knew this by instinct. Ezra had called her name, but she hadn't heard him. This was how he summoned his trifling daughter, seeking her out in the village: *Crack!*

For Mahlon, his friend's terror became his own. When she whirled, her tunic spun higher than a bare thigh, and he saw three scarlet bruises on her white skin, each in the shape of a tanner's framing slat.

"Oh, Milcah," he murmured.

5

"Don't Look for Me in the Morning"

EVEN WHEN THE TIMES ARE AS TROUBLED AS THEY ARE TODAY—
the women, the children, and their feeble grandfathers
left home alone, and no word from the armies north—
Bethlehem goes to work. It has no choice. If the people
allowed worry to overcome labor, a good crop would
fail. What's worse today: all the able-bodied men are
gone. Women must double their efforts to make up the
difference.

And who's surprised when the laggard frets the most?
Ezra is a man, isn't he? Doesn't he own his own field now?
Hasn't he started to build a new house?

But the women make accommodations. Rather than
separating, each to her own duties, they gather. They travel
out to the orchards together. Harvesting, threshing, winnowing, pressing the grapes, it all is lightened by company
and by song.

First to the figs, trees able to survive on stony slopes and undernourished soil. Each woman fills her own basket. The fruit is easily plucked. A gang of hands rises up and goes to work.

Naomi sings, "Once upon a time." She's going to praise heroic women of Israel.

> *Once our locks grew long in Israel,*
> *   so peaceful were our days then,*
> *days when people uncomplaining*
> *   offered their labors each to the others—*
> *   praise the Lord!*

This will be a tale of victory. Therefore:

> *O kings, pay attention! Give ear, you princes!*
> *   To the Lord I will—oh, will I sing,*
> *and tune my voice to the God of Israel!*

In the peace that follows the sunsets, Naomi has often sat and set the base of her harp upon her knee and leaned into the strings and strummed them to the measure of her song. But here, on this particular morning, Naomi sings tunelessly. She casts her voice as harshly as a raven's cry. War and war in the present and the past.

And the women repeat the refrain: "Praise the Lord!"

> *Lord, when you went forth from Seir,*
> *when you marched from the regions of Edom,*
> *   the earth trembled,*
> *   heaven leaped,*
> *   the clouds fell down as water.*

In the days of Sisera, commander of the
    Canaanites,
in the days of Jael, woman whose name
    shall be remembered.
      (Praise the Lord!)

In the days when Canaan oppressed us, oh,
    we abandoned our trade routes,
    traveled in hidden paths,
    deserted our villages,
    crept into caves—
until you, Deborah, prophetess, arose
    as a mother in Israel!
      (Praise the Lord!)

It is possible to pluck figs in unison and to drop them rhythmically into the baskets. In this manner do the women match the cadence of the Hakamah's song.

The sun ascends the eastern sky. Workers begin to sweat. Their mouths grow sticky with thirst.

The early rains won't start for several weeks yet. Yesterday the warriors of Bethlehem carried quantities of water away with them. So the village cistern is nearly empty, its level close to the slime. There is new wine at home, of course, but it has only begun to ferment. And during the celebrations of Sukkoth, which ended on the day that Milcah died, most of the old, stored wines were poured down convivial throats.

So the women make do. Each rubs a pebble clean and sucks it for the moisture saliva produces.

Tell of it,
you who ride on white donkeys.
  Tell of it,
you who sit on woven saddles.
  Tell of it,
all you who walk along the road:
Down to the gates marched Israel,
  frightened, crying,
"Awake! Awake, Deborah! Wake up
  and break into battle song!
"Barak, captain in Israel, arise!
  Take captive your captors,
  O son of Abinoam!"
    (Praise the Lord!)
It was but a remnant marched to the call;
the people of God marched down for him
  against the mighty Canaanite!
  Kings came
  and fought.
The confident kings of Canaan fought
at Taanach by the water of Megiddo.
But they carried off no silver—no!
  nor plunder either—no!

At this charged moment in her story, Naomi breaks off. The fig baskets are full. The Women of Bethlehem swing them each upon her head, and since their hearts beat all as one, they become a single body descending the stony path on soft feet, singing, "Praise the Lord!"

These are not the sweetest figs nor the best to eat fresh.

That batch was plucked in the first harvest, three months ago. This batch is the second harvest, meant mostly for drying in order to preserve them for a winter food. Some will be turned into wine. And Naomi will save a small bag to make a thick syrup for healing skin infections.

Nevertheless, despite this fruit's inferiority, the women sit down in the village square and eat the figs with a little bread dipped in vinegar. The sour bite of the vinegar eases their thirst somewhat; but as much as a third of the women bring fresh goat's milk and share it quickly before it sours in the sun.

While the women rest from their labors, Naomi sings the next chapter of her tale. She creates a driving rhythm to match the riotous speed of the battle:

> *From the heavens the stars themselves did fight,*
> *from their appointed courses they fought against*
>> *Sisera,*
>>> *captain of the Canaanites.*
> *The heavenly hosts stormed and poured down rain.*
> *Then the river Kishon swept our enemies away!*
>> *That rushing torrent,*
>> *the torrents of Kishon!*
> *March on, my soul! Be strong, my sisters!*
>> *(Praise the Lord!)*
>> *Chariots mired.*
>> *Stallions snapped their traces.*
> *Then thundered the horses' hooves,*
> *galloping, galloping, the mighty steeds departing!*
>> *Captain Sisera, fleeing past the woman's tent,*
>> *bethought himself,*

stopped,
returned,
dismounted,
and entered, seeking a place to hide.
"Water," he begged, and Jael,
   Jael gave him milk,
   curds in a lordly bowl.
"Lie down, my lord," she said, "and rest.
I will conceal you under cover of my rug."
   He did and she did
   and he slept.
Jael—O valiant woman!—put her left hand to a
   tent peg
and her right hand to the workman's mallet.
   Sister! Sister, strike!
She struck Sisera through the carpet,
   pierced his temple,
   split his skull.
At her feet he twisted,
   quivering.
At her feet he curled and ceased
   stiffening. Dead.
    (Praise the Lord!)

During the afternoon, the Women of Bethlehem harvest olives. With long sticks they beat the branches. The ripe olives drop like a black rain onto the blankets they've spread below.

Near evening, the wind grows calm because land and sea share an equal temperature. Wearily, the harvesters keep beating the trees and try to clear as many trees as they can before they gather the corners of the blankets together and drag the harvest home.

Naomi has hesitated to sing the last chapter of her tale—for it regards a third woman, she who stayed behind and grieved. The Hakamah, the Wise Woman of Bethlehem, Naomi, has been uncertain of its effect upon her sisters, for this part of the song holds no victory. There are two ways by which the battles of husbands and fathers and sons might end. The one which she hasn't yet unfolded is defeat—when the wives and the mothers who wait at home must wait forever.

But yes. Naomi will sing this too, for this is how she has determined to think about her own men: defeated and perishing.

Deborah, she was first, the commander. Jael, second, the solitary hero. The third is the hero no one will praise. Forever nameless, she is appointed the repository of pain, by whose life, outfacing death, her own people are repaired.

She is the woman at the window, whom artists of every nation have beheld, but always from the outside of her house. And her eyes are always faraway.

She is the mother of Sisera, whose son once commanded the armies of Canaan.

> *"Why is his chariot so tardy in coming?*
> *Why can't I hear them—*
> *why are his hoofbeats delayed?"*
> *So says she to herself, says the mother to herself.*
> *"Perhaps," she thinks, "they're dividing the spoils:*
> *a girl for every warrior,*

colorful robes for my son,
a colorful robe for my neck too,
embroidered,
  the gift of his plunder."
But behold the mother's mouth half-open,
the hope in her eyes and dismay.
Woman at her window
  watching through the lattice,
woman watching, waiting,
  waiting. . . .

BUT THROUGHOUT THE DAY ANOTHER SPIRIT—a military spirit —has been growing behind Naomi's breasts. The military spirit and the home spirit have been wrestling together. Perhaps one part of Naomi can still stay at home. And this part may be the wife of Elimelech and the mother of Mahlon. But the other part is the Mother of Israel—a Deborah who cannot resist the orders of the Lord.

Walk among the wounded.

"Chilion," Naomi says, "don't look for me in the morning."

The two are kneeling at the evening's offering. She has spoken into their silence. Her son must know. He has a right to know, but he cannot come.

Naomi says, "You are in charge of the presses. Let the women bring the olives; but you, son—one by one hang stones as heavy as you can lift on the beam until the oil is pressed out and the vat is full. Take your—" *time,* Naomi is about to say, but Chilion interrupts her.

"I *know*, Mama. I *know* what to do!" Her second son is angry.

Chilion, braver and quicker and more athletic than his older brother. Chilion, so much tougher than tears.

But how capable — my son, my son — capable of a magnificent sulk. It isn't only glory a man receives on the battlefield.

6

Snake-Bit

"DAUGHTER." NAOMI DID NOT USE THE WORD LIGHTLY, this sign of her motherhood. "Daughter," she began to call the child of her heart, and Milcah did not deny her. In fact, she raised her face to the name with open expectations.

And though it is common for an older woman to take the younger under her wing, Milcah's acceptance was the fulfillment of the prayers of a daughterless womb.

"Come, daughter," Naomi said. "Let's sit and drink tea."

They had just come home from the hillsides west of Bethlehem, carrying armloads of herbs and roots, leaves, pods, blossoms, fruit.

"Do you remember which is the wild sage?"

Milcah fingered through the greens spilled out on the courtyard floor. Her gentle pressure produced a riot of pungent smells. Milcah bowed and sniffed and smiled. She selected several spindly stems with long green-greyish leaves and handed them to Naomi.

"See to the fire, child."

While Naomi stuffed the sage into cups, Milcah set

cakes of dried manure on the coals still glowing in the scooped earth, and blew until she'd raised a flame.

Naomi was nearly thirty years old, her complexion leathery, her hands thickened by hard work. She scarcely felt the heat when hanging the copper pot of water close over Milcah's fire. She stood up and went next door for a bottle of sweet date honey. When she returned she paused in the doorway, gazing at the back of this petal-white child tending flames in her courtyard.

Nine years old, her arms and her neck grown more slender than skinny, her hair in such abundance it flowed from under her scarf like a river black and shining, this was a girl approaching womanhood. Milcah: unadorned, wearing the plainest of shifts, but oiled and lissome and lovely and clean, Amen.

Oh, see how dark and even are her eyebrows, and her forehead smooth as alabaster.

Naomi let loops of honey roll into either cup, then poured hot water to the brims, and stirred the wild-sage tea.

"Come up. Sit before I start supper."

Teacher and student, they climbed to the roof and sat and sipped and watched as the faintest sliver of moon traveled down the dark blue sky. Milcah sighed. Naomi recognized the child's reaction to the sweet, piquant tea, for it could sharpen the mind and send the body into waves of relaxation.

Later Naomi would teach the maid how to dry their freshly picked medicinals, how to pound them to powder, grind them with a mortar and pestle, how to make salves, poultices, philters: teach her how to heal.

Greater amounts of sage can tranquilize.

Halfway down the hillsides, down into the lower ravines, grows the fennel that heals infections.

Anemones, thick on the hills in springtime, can cool a fever.

And there is the story that the rod with which Moses split the Red Sea was cut of the wood of the storax tree. Therefore, it is considered a sacred tree—whose gum can heal the ragged wound or still the children's cough.

Oleander fights lice.

Even so, my daughter, even so.

ON ANOTHER SUMMER'S AFTERNOON, while the woman and the girl squatted before two bowls, popping the pods of chickpeas Naomi grew in her kitchen garden, Milcah laughed. One astonishing bark of laughter before she colored and closed her mouth.

Naomi stared.

Why, Milcah had scarcely spoken words to the woman, let alone sentences—but suddenly she allowed some private delight to fly free?

"Milcah!"

Softly: "I'm sorry."

"No, no, no, no, don't be *sorry*, child. It's joy! Your joy makes me joyful!"

Softer still, "Sorry."

"Oh, Milcah." Naomi reduced her voice to the tone of

lullabies. With just the tips of her fingers she touched the back of her daughter's hand. "Milcah, you make me so happy that I want to cry."

"I do?"

Well, well, listen to my mute. This is almost a flood of language!

Naomi took advantage of the moment. She lifted Micah's white hand to her lips and kissed it. "My darling, you've been making me happy for years."

Milcah's eyes rested on the older woman's face—fondly, as it seemed to Naomi.

You can't know the isolations of the Hakamah. How could you know her pleasure in your presence?

Aloud she said, "Only one or two chickpeas to a pod. Better we keep working."

When their bowls were full Naomi scooped out enough to give the five people of her family snacks for several days. These she placed in the oven to roast. The rest she would dry in the sun.

They gathered the pods in their skirts and carried them out to a hole which Elimelech's father had cut in bedrock. There they dumped the green shells and covered the hole again with a flagstone: silage for the cattle.

The roasted peas began to crackle. Milcah swept them from the oven. Naomi salted them. They brewed wild-sage tea and went upstairs to sit.

Milcah didn't laugh again. But while they sat together, Naomi noticed a twinkling in her eyes.

"Something's funny?"

As easily as the caper flower opens to the evening, Milcah said, "Papa."

Naomi turned a full gaze on her daughter. "Ezra?"

"Snakebite," Milcah said, then hiccoughed, trying to control the joke. In a voice melodic with a glee, she said, "Little baby snake fell out of the ceiling last night. Landed in Papa's mouth—" Tears began to roll down her cheeks. Milcah fairly squealed: "He woke up. Papa woke up slapping his face. He gagged and spit and spat and passed a baby snake! Oh, oh!"

Milcah was hurting herself with laughter. Naomi could scarcely believe the beauty of the day.

Ezra! Ezra the tanner!

Milcah said, "I gave him blackberry berries to suck on."

7

Oiled and Salted

IN THE COLDEST NIGHT OF THE WINTER, Naomi crept close to Ezra's hovel.

"Milcah?" beneath a window, keeping her voice low.

And from inside: "Yes?"

"It's time."

Naomi slung a large bag over her shoulder and hurried through the crooked lanes to Salmon's house. The wind was freshening in the west. Clouds blackened that half of the sky, killing its stars.

At the house she pushed the door into an interior room. The air was warm and heavy with human exhalations. The wind flickered the flames of three lamps until the door was closed. Two women sat against the back wall. A third paced restlessly, groaning and holding up her huge belly with two hands. It seemed that her arms were too weary to carry her womb.

Naomi dropped the bag to the floor. "Come," she said. "Miriam," she said. "Lie down and let me measure you."

She eased the laboring woman to a freshly woven pallet,

then laid her back. Naomi at midwifery: she washed her hands in water simmering outside the door.

"Bend your knees."

Naomi lifted the hem of Miriam's shift and rolled it up against the great, laden belly. She drew a small flask from her bag, then slipped a hand between Miriam's thighs. "Spread them." She moistened her fingers with the olive oil, then anointed the tender membranes of Miriam's vulva.

Slowly she worked her fingers in. "Four fingers wide," she announced. "It's your first, Miriam. We'll have to wait a while."

The door opened. Milcah slipped into the room. Her woolen robe was dotted with the first fat drops of rain. She tossed it into a corner.

Fearful father Salmon was squatting in the room he had built on his roof, his hands hanging over his kneecaps. Other men would soon tromp up to sit with him. Elimelech, of course. Ephrathites like himself. His son, Boaz.

He had carried up several containers of beer to help pass the night in fellowship. He himself was too preoccupied to drink or even to talk. Miriam was his second wife, so young, so untried, in danger of death. Too many women perished on the birthing board. Salmon's first wife. She had died giving life to Boaz sixteen years ago.

> The day I bore fruit, how happy I was, happy was I,
>   my husband.
> The day of my laboring, my face darkened.
> The day of my giving birth, my eyes clouded.
> With open hands I prayed, Save my life!

Husband, you uttered a cry:
"Why do you take my wife?"
Many days was I beside you, my husband.
I lived with my lover.
Death came creeping into my bedroom.
It drove me from my house.
It tore me from my husband.

Naomi knows the fears of the men. This business belongs to women. Men can do nothing. Awkward as donkeys, yet Naomi felt no scorn. She sympathized. Their suffering was their helplessness. It was partly on their account she strove for a successful birth.

"Oh! Oh! Eeeeeeeeeeeee!"

Miriam hunched up and forward.

Naomi turned to one of the women in the room, to Miriam's mother she said: "Rizpah, get the birthing board."

Rizpah stood and went out.

Milcah took Naomi's flask of oil, poured a small pool on Miriam's magnificent belly, and massaged it, massaged it till their skins shared heat together.

At the same time Naomi stirred fennel powder into a cup of honeyed wine. As the contraction passed, she held the cup to Miriam's closed mouth. She touched the tip of her finger to the surface of the wine and let one drop fall into the line between her lips, moistening it from corner to corner. Miriam licked the wine. Naomi tilted the cup, and Miriam drank.

"It's to strengthen your labors. The fennel will open your womb."

All at once they heard Rizpah yelling outside: "Get away! Get away!"

The birthing board came with a sudden thrust through the door. Behind it followed not Rizpah, but a man. He swung the board like a club. Boaz, Salmon's son.

Milcah shrieked, dropped the oil flask, and jumped for her robe.

Rizpah rushed in with an oxgoad, but couldn't bring herself to swing it.

Young Boaz bulked in the small room. He threw down the board beside Miriam. Seventeen years old, tall for his age, he exuded a male scent. The door stood open. The cold wind cut the woman-warmth, and the oil lamps guttered.

"You! Boaz," Naomi flared like a cobra. "This is a holy place. These are holy things."

He glared down at Miriam, breathing heavily. "I just want to see."

Milcah swept her robe over Miriam's nakedness.

"Perversion!" Rizpah cried.

But there was nothing juvenile in Boaz's expression. Naomi saw scrutiny instead, and then contempt, the face of every male who thought he had the right to dominate.

Naomi hissed, "If you don't take your manself out of here, boy, I will curse you. I will curse you in the name of Lilith, and you *will be* cursed."

The room fell into a hush.

Boaz compressed his lips. He snatched the oxgoad from Rizpah's hand and whacked the doorframe and left.

There passed a brief, breathless silence. Then Miriam

reasserted the dreadful holiness of the moment by raising a red streak of screaming. All four women went to work.

Rizpah, Miriam's mother, set the board up and began to wipe it clean.

Miriam's aunt wrapped a tough rope around the ceiling beam directly over the birthing board. She let both ends hang down. Woven into each end was a soft leather loop. She sprinkled a fresh, loamy earth on the ground below the angle cut into the lower part of the board.

Milcah supported Miriam's shoulders through another contraction.

When it passed and the poor woman lay back almost blind with sweat, Naomi cooed and purred and reached to make another examination.

"Eight fingers," she said softly. "Soon, daughter." She kissed Miriam's forehead. "You are so worthy, so noble and worthy."

To the rest she said, "Help me."

In concert the four women grabbed hold of the corners of the blanket, and lifted Miriam, and carried her to the birthing board, and lay her on its angled descent, and wrapped the blanket over her. The baby would be born through the V sawn upside-down in the lower portion of the board. It opened into two wooden legs at the ground.

Naomi took her harp from the bag and sat on a three legged stool.

Everything was ready.

The whole board was covered in sheeps' hides. Miriam's knees would be drawn up, her heels pressing against blocks left and right and close to her buttocks.

Milcah tied a clean cloth into a knot, soaked it in the fennel wine, and laid it across Miriam's open mouth.

The midwife sang:

> *When the Lord swore to Sarah, barren,*
> *that she would bear a son,*
> *old age and Abraham's older age*
> *caused her to laugh.*

Miriam set her teeth. She frowned, her eyebrows crushing her eyes. She hunched her shoulders, wailed and wailed and sank back. Milcah wiped her face.

Naomi paused, watchful. Then continued more cautiously:

> *God said, "Why is she laughing?*
> *Is anything too wonderful for me?"*

Naomi's attentions were fully on Miriam. Time.... Time....

> *The Lord dealt with Sarah as he had said;*
> *he did for her as he had promised—*

Thunder cracked. Rain beat hard on Salmon's house.

Miriam grabbed the two leather loops, and hauled herself halfway up from the plank behind her. "Oh, God!" she shouted. "Oh, God, God!"—louder than the storm outside.

Naomi swung her stool inside the legs of the board, between the knees of the woman in delivery. The skull was bulging through its mother's flesh. Naomi put her right palm against the skull, and cupped her left hand under the opening.

"Milcah," Naomi said. "Her shoulders."

The midwife's apprentice ran her arms under both Miriam's shoulders, and let this mother spend all her energies pushing.

Then, just as the squashed forehead began to squeeze forth, Naomi seized the baby's crown with the points of her fingers, tenderly turning it, tugging—and with a slurping sound the baby squirted into the universe, chalky, blue, its mouth skewed open on a soundless howl.

It wasn't breathing.

A hand under its butt, a hand to cradle its back and two fingers for the little head, Naomi raised the baby, its face in front of her own face. She blew a sharp puff into its nostrils, and oh how that tiny body clenched and the little elbows trembled. Oh *my*, what marvelous defiance she cried to great creation: *I am here! I am here!*

Salmon, you have a baby girl.

It was Milcah who oiled and salted the infant and wrapped her in bands of a womb-like wool; Milcah who brought a clean warm rag to Naomi.

The four of them had been left alone: the midwife and her apprentice, Miriam and her willful baby girl. The storm had passed. Soon day would break.

Miriam hadn't been moved from the birthing board. Her lips so dry, they cracked. Her body so exhausted the joints were loose, all of them unknotted. Her eyes were closed, her eyebrows high, and her chin reposed in sleep.

Neither had Naomi moved. She watched and waited between the mother's knees. "Little sister, come out," she crooned on her three-legged stool. "No need to dally."

But in fact the placenta *had* delayed almost four hours by now. Miriam needed to rest on the pallet. And there were a few things left to be done before the sun arose.

"Milcah," Naomi said. "A little pepper?"

The girl herself had nodded off. No blame for that. She was just eleven.

"Get the pepper from my bag."

So Milcah shook a few grains of ground peppercorn onto the backs of her knuckles. She brought them to Miriam's nose and tipped the grains in a nostril.

Whoops! The young mother sniffed, inhaled, and exploded in a beautiful sneeze. Out shot the afterbirth. Naomi caught it.

"Welcome, little sister!"

Together they helped Miriam down to her bed, and the baby beside her, and beside the baby the placenta, its umbilical uncut. Even so would the silent sister lend the newborn hope through the first hours of the infant's life.

In the morning, after she was well awake, Miriam gave Naomi the little pouch which she had embroidered for this occasion — as long as her baby was born alive.

Now, then, Naomi cut the cord. Miriam clothed the afterbirth in its little pouch. Milcah carried it tenderly out into the courtyard, to a circle of earth which surrounded the stump of an ancient fig tree. Milcah of the white hands knelt down and dug through the earth. Milcah buried the little sister. Milcah had been given this task, that she might learn a tremendous verity: for even as the afterbirth must enter the ground today, so shall the baby born go down into the ground tomorrow.

SEVEN NIGHTS LATER, WHEN ALL was well—the mother's milk generously flowing, the baby's mouth a capable sucker, her tiny body flourishing, and her future life a probable prospect—Miriam whispered, "Basemath."

For Basemath means "Balsam," and *that* was the cord of their kinship ever thereafter, as long as either one of them continued to live.

"O baby, O Basemath, O child of mine, you are my Balm."

8

The First Day of the War

THE WARRIORS OF BENJAMIN ARE FAMOUS FOR THE DELIGHT they take in warfare. Broad-headed men, stout on their feet, their centers of gravity set so low that they might roll at the first crack of a battleax—they won't go down. Their armies race across the fields like the shadow of a dark cloud coming, and like wild boars they pepper through the forests, their short necks rigid.

With seven hundred picked men the Benjamites can outfight forces ten times their size. They are ambidextrous, fighting lefthanded to the enemy's right, or right to his left. Moreover, every one of the seven hundred champions is so skilled with the sling, he can whirl his stone at a sparrow in flight and kill it in a single shot.

HOW, O LORD, SHALL WE PROCEED? The chiefs of the eleven tribes have gathered at Mizpah. They put the inquiry to the Levite in their midst, charging him to beg heaven for an answer. And the Levite—whose wretchedness has gal-

vanized the hearts of the armies—performs his office. He
sets aside his personal grief and takes up both the ephod
and his teraphim, asking: *Which tribe shall go up first to
battle against the Benjamites?*

The chiefs sit in a circle, their shoulders wrapped
against the chill of the night. Beyond their tight enclosure,
so many fires are flickering they look like heaven's stars
spread out on the earth. Tents lie in the firelight like an
endless herd of sleeping cattle. In the valleys, up and over
the hillsides, as far off as the fields of Ephraim the armies
of Israel have established their camps. Silence awaits their
morning orders. Now and again a guard shouts out, and
then a jackal yaps.

Finally the Levite interprets the will of the Lord. The
Lord says: *Judah shall go up first.*

BEFORE THE DAWN'S LIGHT THE CHIEFS send messengers to
their captains. One by one the captains sing out their
commands—individual, bodiless voices crying across the
countryside, waking the soldiers to their task.

The men are too intense to talk. They make a mechani-
cal noise in the camps. It's the cinching of leather in metal,
bridles, the slow crunch of supply wagons, boxes snapped
open and shut again, weapons clattering, boots and bare
feet shuffling.

Judah goes out first, in a great swath crushing the
dew-grasses black behind them. Judah moves as quietly
as it can from Mizpah the five miles to Gibeah. There is
a route they might have marched south through Ramah,

but it offers no cover. They move the more slowly through wood.

On a field close to the city, Salmon raises the ram's horn to his mouth and shatters the sunrise. Immediately the troops break into a sprint, foot soldiers roaring and massing in the front. In the back of the charging army bowmen halt and release a storm-cloud of arrows. Arrows stream the skies. They arc over Judah, then angle down on the men of Benjamin already in battle formation outside the city of Gibeah.

The Benjamites raise short shields to cover their heads. Here and there an arrow pierces through and bites a warrior. But another man steps into his place, and the battle line holds true. They can be patient, the armies of Benjamin, because they are confident. No warrior will jump too soon, none will fall back in fear. Everyone trusts his neighbor. Wait, wait, wait ... *now!*

Galloping, leaping the thickets like antelopes, Judah hurls javelins and spins sling-stones round their heads, trying to weaken the foe so that the shock of the infantry shatters him. Trying—but failing.

For Judah hasn't run unharried. Men fall by the stones that crack their skulls. Others trip over the corpses to be driven headlong down. Some who have flashed past the casualties now catch glimpses of the lines before them and suffer second thoughts.

And then *(O you hosts of the Lord!)* the clash.

Judah attacks its little brother Benjamin. Wave after wave, the foot soldiers throw themselves against the battle lines of the enemy. Armed with spears, sickle swords, war-clubs, their eyes white with fury, throats roaring like the wild bear's—from the north of the morning to the south of it—Judah crashes against this human headland. But Benjamin remains unmoved. Four hundred Judeans fall on the points of Benjamin's spears. Then, slipping in a bloody mud, men rise to confront each other. Warriors strive so close-shouldered that one man catches spittle blown from another man's panting. Hand to hand. Whiskers grinding into another's neck. Grunting, cursing. A stout warrior loops his arms around his enemy and heaves him from the ground and slams his back down hard enough to break the spine. Wide-eyed, the dead man doesn't die. Short, quick stabs of the dagger. Fists split flesh along the jawbone. Hands lock on a wounded man's throat. And so, and so....

Benjamin never breaks. He withstands the attack as if he were stone.

At noonday Salmon rides a white donkey back and forth behind the failing armies of Judah. He curls his fingers into the ram's horn and wails the signal for retreat.

As the Judeans lumber and limp toward the rear, the rest of Israel passes them at a quick-march to Gibeah.

"Hey, Cousin! You soften 'em up for me?"

But this cousin hasn't the breath to answer. The best of the fresh troops are baffled. It seems to the Judeans that the fresh troops hold them in contempt.

But Benjamin is famous for his vindications.

By the end of the first day of fighting, all eleven tribes of Israel have been repulsed. None touched Gibeah. The Israelite chiefs who go down to survey the evening battlefields count twenty-two thousand bodies.

Tonight they transfer their headquarters from Mizpah to Bethel, two-and-a-half miles farther north—but with good reason. The sanctuary of the Ark of the Covenant rests in Bethel. It is here, then, before this more glorious shrine, that the chiefs fall on their faces. Oh, God!— haven't we obeyed the Lord in every particular? *Judah shall go first.* And Judah did go first. What went wrong? What could *they* have done wrong?

Surely their cause is just. Surely Gibeah deserves the chastisement of the right arm of the Almighty. Benjamin has chosen to defend the wicked! Wickedness must not prevail. God knows the ways of the unrighteous. Surely the ways of Gibeah reek in his holy nostrils!

THIS IS THE STORY THE LEVITE told the tribes of Israel as soon as they had all assembled in Mizpah last night. The Levite, a grossly heavy man, took a stance in a great hollow of rock. His face trembling, his voice orotund and grave, all men were moved by the horrors he had suffered.

It became the testimony by which the chiefs of Israel justified their wars:

We left Bethlehem in the afternoon, the Levite began. *Three days ago we set out for Ephraim, I and my servant and my wife. And I made sure that Milcah rode in comfort on my well-trained donkey.*

He paused. He laid a beringed finger to the side of his nose.

At twilight we passed by the city of Jebus. My servant said we should turn in, but everyone knows it's a city of foreigners. We rode on.

Then we saw the fires of Gibeah. "There," I said. "That's a town of our brother Benjamin." We turned in there.

Oh, my lords, don't blame me if I utter my words in anger.

That night men of Gibeah surrounded the house where we were sleeping! They wanted to kill me! All of us! They raped my wife instead, and she is dead.

What else should a sanctified man and a loving husband do? 'Twas an abomination! Lascivious! Malicious! What was there for me to do but cut my wife into pieces and send the corpse of this horror to all the tribes of Israel?

When the Levite had finished, the chiefs rose up as one man, and swore their devotion: "Not one warrior will return to his house," they announced. "We'll go up against Gibeah by lot. A thousand men in ten thousand, a hundred in a thousand, we will execute judgment upon his savagery."

YET DESPITE THE RIGHTEOUSNESS OF the purposes of the chiefs of Israel, today eleven tribes were thrown back by one. Benjamin.

And so it is that the chiefs are pressing their foreheads against the flagstones before the Ark of the Covenant, rocking, moaning, and weeping the supplicant's tears.

Israel will no longer seek the Lord's will by means of the Levite, his ephod and his teraphim. Something is eating away at the man. He's gone off into the shadows.

The sanctuary at Bethel has its own priest, a Levite

himself and a man of impeccable heritage. He is Phinehas, the son of Eleazar, the grandson of Aaron — grandson of the Aaron who served the children of Israel in the wilderness beside his brother Moses.

Phinehas inquires of the Lord: "Shall we again draw near to the battle against our brother Benjamin?"

And the Lord God answers, *Go up against them.*

AT SUNRISE THE FOLLOWING MORNING Naomi staggers to the top of a stony ridge. Spread across the valleys and the hills before her is a great apron of human clutter. The camps and the tents of Israel, yes — but none of its good order. Staves have fallen flat. Jars roll back and forth in the same wind that causes tent flaps to billow and to reach up like sleeves. Broken weapons have been thrown like bones into piles. Otherwise there is a great, whistling quiet.

She descends the ridge, limping.

Naomi left Bethlehem eight hours ago. It was her plan to arrive here before the armies marched. The war could not have been won in a single day, or she'd have met victors on the roads. On the other hand, she has had every right to believe in the health of her people. The odds are eleven to one. The odds belong to the good that struggles against the evil. But this, the state of the camps — this dismays her.

Naomi is late arriving. The large bag slung sideways over her back has troubled her left leg. And because of the tardiness, she comes with more anxiety than a Hakamah should.

The muddy paths in Israel's camps are splotted with

blood. Blood has pooled on pallets inside the yawning tents.

There were wounded here! Where are the wounded?

Naomi considers dropping the healer's bag by a tent in the center of the camps. She planned to treat the wounded in a single location. Now she changes her mind. She will have to carry the bag to the wounded—wherever they are.

Curse this leg! She wants to *run*.

Suddenly she sees a human form ahead—sitting on a casement at the camp's southeastern gate. But he isn't dressed like a soldier.

"Hello? Sir? Hello?"

The man doesn't hear.

When he stands and starts to wander away, Naomi does drop the bag and picks up her speed.

"Sir! I want to talk with you!"

The man turns—and Naomi stops, flooded with pity. It's the Levite.

"Oh," she says, "I'm sorry."

The widower is mourning. He has suffered a terrible loss. But ... didn't he have the strength three days ago to call all Israel together? Today he stares at the ground, puffing his cheeks and sighing. He answers her by a shrug of his shoulders. Just now the Levite looks like a criminal broken by a load of iniquity.

Naomi's first instinct is to sing an incantation and to feed him. And she might have—except that the ram's horn starts tearing the air south of the camps: *Charge!*

She grabs the Levite's arm. "Where are the wounded?"

She shakes him. "Levite! Where are the wounded?"

"In wagons," he mumbles without emotion.

"Gone where?"

"With the armies."

"Into battle?"

A shrug. He pulls himself free.

She stands astounded. *What fool would*—? "Levite! In God's name, *why?*"

"Everybody's gone to war."

"Even the injured?"

The Levite snaps up straight. He raises a premonitory finger as if listening to the wind, then speaks in the tones of dreadful mystery: "The Lord said through me: *Let Judah go first.* But Judah retreated. Israel retreated. Benjamin gave the lie to the God of Abraham. Or else ..." The finger falls. The Levite droops and walks off, saying, "The Lord God hates me. *Go up against them,* he said again last night, as if he'd never said it first through me."

The earth has begun to tremble. The army is charging. The earth opens its throat and roars in a hundred thousand voices.

As well as she might, Naomi hefts her bag. Painfully, she hurries forward.

For the Lord God may have said to the chiefs of Israel: *Go up.* But he did not add: *And I will give them into your hand.*

9

Nine Months before the War

WHEN THE PREACHER CAME TO TOWN on two handsome donkeys, one for baggage and the other for his considerable person, he saluted the people without dismounting. He waved his hands above their heads in blessing, then indicated to the chiefs that they would enjoy his benefits for two weeks before he passed on to other villages in Judah.

He had ridden here, he said, from the hill country of Ephraim.

That same day he moved himself into the house of a citizen, spent water on his ablutions, ate well, slept well, then began to preach.

"In the darkest place, in the holiest place, there rests the Ark of the Covenant, mysterious and mighty, which Moses once constructed of acacia wood while the children of Israel moved as nomads through the wilderness."

His voice was a resonant, roar-like organ, whether he stood outside in the village square or sat on the roof of some substantial farmer. The man himself was opulent, a most inspiring Levite. He clothed himself in fine white linen robes whose tassels had been dyed in purple. His slippers were of the Anatolian style, the toes turned up. And his turban was wonderfully Mesopotamian. A tooled bronze serpent coiled around his upper arm—pressed into the flesh of the arm, actually, for he was a man of girth.

"Housed in the sanctuary at Bethel in Ephraim and in an impenetrable darkness," the Levite intoned, "sits the God of Abraham and Isaac and Jacob, upon the Mercy Seat, between the Cherubim, in the midst of his people."

Presently the Levite was abiding in Elimelech's house. He slept upon a bed framed with wood and under-slung with ropes. There was only one such bed in Bethlehem, but a man who could access the voice of the Lord by means of the ephod and the teraphim, a man who knew Torah, was worthy of the best the peasants had to offer.

Recognizing the Levite's capacities for food, Naomi prepared heaps of savory dishes. Nor did she hesitate to stand as the only woman among the men who listened while he taught. Naomi learned, and Milcah of the white hands served. It took a foreigner truly to measure the modesty and the grace of her service. And since she kept her eyes cast down, her hair a marvelous rain from under her scarf, that man might stare without fear of embarrassment—and all the while keep preaching.

"For who can know the mind of the Creator? Who can see his glory and not go blind? Who can enter his presence and not perish?"

When the great man had finished imparting knowledge to the willing, there were only five left in Elimelech's room, sitting on rugs around a freshly woven mat, enjoying an evening meal. They were Elimelech and his two sons, his wife, and, prominently, the Levite. They watched in a respectful silence as Milcah knelt and set bowls of fruits and cheeses on the mat.

"Milcah," Naomi said, pointing to an empty cup, "the Levite."

The young woman bowed and went downstairs for another skin of wine.

"Milcah," the Levite said, folding his hands over his belly. "So pleasing to the sight. Hmm."

Elimelech said with pride, "And better than that—loyal. Trustworthy. Our daughter works with willing hands."

"I wonder," the Levite mused as if to himself, "how old the girl could be."

Naomi said, "Fifteen—"

"A daughter fifteen and ready for—"

Elimelech jumped on his word: "No, sir, not the daughter of our blood—"

"Elimelech!" Naomi interrupted. To the Levite: "The dearest daughter of my heart!"

Despite the speed of his hosts' dialogue, the Levite continued at the same pace, like a slowly rolling stone: "Hmm. Then. I wonder: who is the true father—I mean, of course, the blood father—of this jasper, this precious jewel."

Elimelech said, "Ezra—"

Naomi snapped, "Ezra, a tanner! A miserable excuse for a *man*, let alone a father."

Elimelech said, "You won't find love there. My wife is the one who taught her love. Milcah loves Naomi."

Naomi looked at the Levite with defiance, as if an interloper might dispute Elimelech's word.

But he didn't. He turned and regarded her a moment, then burst into a florid smile, his cheeks and his chins wreathing round with radiance. "If such a young thing loves you, lady, it is beauty that springs from the beauty in you, and generosity that shapes *your* love."

"Ah!" Naomi was startled by the generosity of his compliment. Defiance melted, and gratitude bloomed in the wrinkles of her face.

The Levite touched two fingers to his forehead. "I bow to your discernment as well as to the child of your maternal, enrapturing heart."

And so it was that the Levite from Ephraim stayed two weeks more in Bethlehem, every night in Elimelech's house under the benign eyes of his wife, who permitted her daughter sometimes to sit in the shadows while a woman and a man spoke of Torah and obedience.

ONCE WHEN NAOMI WAS A CHILD, her father decided to dig a grain-pit in his courtyard close to the oven and the cookfires. Three of his neighbors helped cart the stones from his fields to his house. Her father had drawn a circle with chalk on the courtyard floor. There the four men worked their shovels and rounded out a three-foot hole. Next they heaved stones in to cover the bottom and build up the sides.

But the oldest neighbor dropped headfirst into the pit and pitched about so wildly, he whacked his skull and scraped his elbows against the stone. He foamed at his mouth, ground his teeth and gabbled nonsense.

The poor fellow had always lived in Bethlehem. But he was Rosh, a Benjamite, and Naomi wondered if madness ran in the blood of that tribe.

Two of the workers jumped back and hissed spells. Naomi watched with a kind of horrid fascination. Her father stood still.

"Papa, stop him."

"Can't, girl. Rosh'll stop on his own. He has these fits two, three times a year."

It happened as her father said. The man ceased his rant. His lids lowered halfway and he seemed to slumber. Naomi could not turn her eyes away. When Rosh blinked and focused on her, the girl said, "You talked."

"I did?" The man cleared his throat. "What did I say?"

"Mr. Rosh, don't *you* know what you said?"

After that first experience, the healer came to recognize the same symptoms in other people, which meant that, however uncommon, this was an affliction suffered by more than one man and more than one tribe.

As Naomi grew in stature and in the practices of a healer, she asked others how to treat this falling disease. No one knew. Mostly it scared people. They avoided those who collapsed in fits, and then remembered nothing of the experience.

After several years of frustration, Naomi met a woman from Gilead who taught her an incantation to be chanted over the convulsions themselves:

Adjured are you, spirit, in the name of the Lord and in the

name of his holy angels, to be expelled and keep from Rosh!
You no longer have power over him. Be bound by the chains
of the sea ever farther from him.

The illness was seldom seen in Bethlehem. Naomi came upon it twice while in her twenties. Both times she used the old woman's incantation, but in neither instance did it defy the convulsions, keep them from returning. So the young healer questioned the chant and its presumptions. What if she were with something mightier than mere spirits?

A traveler from the Land Between the Rivers who said that he was an *Ashipu*, a doctor among the Children of Aram, offered Naomi another remedy.

Well, "remedy" wasn't the best word for this treatment. "Exorcism" was. For the *Ashipu* believed that the convulsions were caused by "the hand," as he put it, of a demon. Foul substances would purify a man bedeviled by *most* maladies. But this required measures more dire. Trick the demon out of its human nest, then capture it in solutions so noxious the wicked spirit is sapped of its strength.

"Cut off the little finger of a dead man," the *Ashipu* instructed. "Lay it to one side. Make a small pouch from the skin of a virgin goat. Mix copper filings with rancid oil. Pour them into your pouch, then drop the severed finger in too."

Naomi listened to the prescription with no disgust for its materials. It was the diagnosis that left her cold. Demons? Among us there is but one God: the Lord.

The man noticed Naomi's lapse of attention. In his lugubrious accent he continued. "Drop the dead finger into the oily corruption. Draw the neck of your pouch closed with the beard-hairs of a thief. String the pouch on the tendon of a gerbil, and hang the whole around the convulsive's neck. He will recover."

Naomi thanked the Aramean with cakes and raisins. She bade him farewell for good and dismissed his formula. Not that it wouldn't work elsewhere. She'd never deny another nation's god his power. But Naomi did not worship gods who were not the God of Abraham, Isaac, and Jacob.

Hear, O Israel, the Lord our God, the Lord is one.

Whatever was visited upon his chosen people, it came from the hand of the Lord. Cursings or blessings, either one. And if there were spirits involved, it was always and only the Spirit of Israel's God, his breath, his wind, the force of his own existence.

Finally Naomi could no longer accept that this affliction was a chastisement of the Lord. And if a visitation be Godly, why try to drive it away?

The Hakamah of Bethlehem had begun to see in these convulsions a sacred ecstasy, and to hear in the gabbling the fragments of divinity.

Behold, I have put my words in your mouth. Whatever I command you, you shall speak.

WHO ASKS A YOUNG WOMAN whether she *wants* to be married to that man or this? Did Jacob ask Rachel if she wished to marry him? No. The desire of his heart was reason enough. Did Laban sit down with his daughter Leah to ask her opinion in the matter of marrying Jacob? Of course not, even though the sisters argued bitterly thereafter.

Parents choose. Parents negotiate the prices involved: a dowry for the husband from the father of the bride; and a *mohar* paid by the husband to the father for the loss of his daughter's service.

Yet, in spite of the fixed tradition, Naomi said to Milcah, "Talk to me."

They sat in Elimelech's upper room, sipping warm sage-and-honey tea, their robes pulled tight against the wet winter chill.

Here is the sort of intimacy these women shared: not only that Naomi would ask after her daughter's feelings, but also that she, Milcah, answered:

"Papa hasn't beaten me in two years. Things are better at home."

"But your life would improve with the Levite."

It was Naomi's habit to strike down on the last words of someone else's sentences, whereas Milcah paused constantly, considering the thought before she spoke it. "Who would tend to Papa? Feed him, sweep the house, massage his joints, cut his toenails?"

"Bethlehem doesn't want for kind people."

"Naomi. You know. There's no one but me."

"*And* me," Naomi said. "I can rub a man's arthritis. Drink your tea."

The younger woman bowed her face and sipped liquid from her cup. Then, pressing its warmth against her cheek, she said, "Every time he thinks about you he spits."

"Right. A stupid idea—though he might change his mind if he gets desperate."

Milcah's meditations didn't change. "The only reason he lets me come to you is, he wants what I bring home."

Naomi called these generosities "wages." Ezra called them, "Mine." And so long as everything else stayed the same—Milcah's availability and his comfort—he let his "ewe lamb loose to run the streets."

Naomi said, "He doesn't beat you. But he screams at you. He curses your eyes. Turns your good days into miseries. Oh, child, how often I've held you in my arms while you sobbed it out."

Milcah of the white hands said, "Oh, I would miss you. How could I go without you?"

A surge of feeling constricted Naomi's throat. She gave her head an angry shake.

"He's got good points—the Levite, I mean. He doesn't stink. He owns two donkeys and good linen and a respectable livelihood and, look: he travels nine months out of a year. The man pulls God behind him like a kite."

The image struck them both as funny. A man running and yanking at a thin string. Milcah stole a glance at Naomi, grinning.

Naomi took advantage of the moment. "I think he'll make a responsible husband, don't you? A merciful turn of mind. When have we *ever* met a man more magnanimous with a finer tongue than his? Milcah, this marriage will be a blessed elevation."

"He *is* a gentle man," the young woman said. "Always

polite. And always respectful of me. His fingernails are clean. Yet he never mentions the grime in mine."

"Why should he? To him you are as pleasant as pomegranates."

Naomi heard foot-stomping in the courtyard, then Chilion's brassy cackle.

She couldn't tell whether Milcah heard the men below. Though the girl was a mere fifteen years, she looked more solemn than her years.

Milcah said, "He already has a wife."

"I know that! But he has no children, Milcah! The wife that bears his child is the wife he will adore."

Softer still, Milcah said: "That's not the worst."

"Worst what? What do you think is the worst?"

"We said it already. Papa will never let me go. Five months ago a man came to the house to speak for me. Papa cursed him with such fury, it set my papa's face on fire. That was the last man—"

"I know no such thing!"

"But Naomi, it's true—"

"That Ezra will never let you go? No, it's not true."

Naomi stood up and went through the door onto the open roof. "Elimelech! Come here! A girl needs good news!" She turned to Milcah, her countenance folded into ruts of gladness. "Here, my dear one, let me pour you a little more tea."

It was the *mohar* that exercised Ezra's soul.

Days before Naomi's conversation with Milcah, the

Levite had suggested they negotiate with Milcah's father in Elimelech's house rather than in the tanner's.

"We wouldn't want to shame a man in a hovel," he said.

So the three men sat cross-legged in a private room discussing marriage. Two of them expected to spend an hour or more chatting about everything *except* the matter that had brought them together. But Ezra cared nothing for ceremony.

"What's the offer," he said, scratching the whiskers above his Adam's apple.

The Levite was stunned out of speech.

Elimelech thought that his role as a mediator had already been fulfilled. He'd spoken to Ezra on behalf of the Levite. He had persuaded Ezra that the worthy Ephraimite was in earnest. No one meant to dupe a poor tanner. Yes, and they both understood what a tremendous value Milcah was for her father—or else why would a man of sacerdotal standing hold the daughter in such high regard? So Ezra had accepted Elimelech's invitation and now was leaping past protocol, asking, "What's the offer?"

When he saw the Levite's speechlessness, Elimelech followed tradition and started low. "What do you think of the armlet the Levite wears? An expensive serpent tooled in bronze. Look closely. It's eyes are tiny carnelians."

Ezra put his palms to the floor and pushed himself halfway to standing: stringy muscles in his bare arms, arrogance in the lift of his pitiful eyebrows.

The Levite found his tongue.

"No, no, no, our good host knows not my mind. Sit

down. Of *course* a clever fellow would never be satisfied with a trinket."

"Right. I got a eye for tricks and truths."

"Well, then." The Levite linked fingers over his belly and nodded sagely. "What, I wonder, would a clever businessman think an appropriate *mohar* might be?"

"A wheat field."

"Oh! Well! Yes.... A wheat field. Hmm."

"Can't eat your snake. Can't sell it. Not in Bethlehem. And what's the good if I could? A tanner needs somethin' that'll *keep* payin' him, y'understand. Year in, year out. No more'n no less than the work his daughter does, year in, year out." Ezra blinked by a rapid twitching of his whole face. "He's losin' th' only family he has. His sightly child." Ezra sighed. "His beautiful baby."

"Sightly," said the Levite. "Beautiful."

"Prettiest, kindliest, most dutiful, smartest—and downright, break-my-heart *beautiful!*"

A film of water washed the Levite's eyes. Softly he said, "Beautiful."

And the tanner said, "A wheat field."

Milcah's suitor pressed a finger to his bibulous lips and, sweating, promised the tanner a wheat field. Immediately Ezra was swimming in the oils of everlasting friendship and thanksgivings.

As the satisfied business man legged it from the room, Elimelech noticed his wife, who had been listening around the corner from the door.

The Levite sat exceedingly still.

Elimelech said, "You've gotten your heart's desire. Why aren't you celebrating?"

"Well," the Levite murmured, "a wheat field."

"A hard bargain, but a bargain."

"Yes, but we didn't mention *where* this field might be. Perhaps her father thinks he'll follow me to Ephraim—"

Elimelech said, "That's what *I* thought. You've got fields in Ephraim, right?"

"Ah. Hmm." The Levite pondered the question, then lifted his lip in a fleeting grin. "Well, of course I do."

"Then where's the problem?"

"Elimelech!" Naomi stepped into the room. "Milcah needs to get *away* from that wretch. There's your problem."

"Yes!" the Levite nodded vigorously. "Who *wouldn't* worry for the gentle woman's peace of mind?"

"We can fix that," Elimelech said. "Give Ezra silver enough to purchase the field here, then ride off free of the long-toothed rat."

The Levite lost enthusiasm. "It's a good plan—if I had the silver," he said.

Naomi pinched her husband. "Don't be so blithe about serious things."

"Naomi!"

The Levite sighed. "As you both know, I came unprepared to marry. I brought no silver with me."

"Then I've run clean out of ideas." Elimelech stood and stretched. "Call it off, find a good woman—"

Naomi pinched him again.

"Stop that, woman!"

Naomi said, "We have the field."

"What?"

"We *have* a field," she said. She squatted and spoke to the Levite. "How long before you can return with payment for the loan of Elimelech's field?"

"Naomi!"

"Hush, you ... man."

The Levite beamed. "Six months! Eight months anyway. Usually it would take me two years to make my circuit through Israel—"

"Stop this!" Elimelech shouted.

"—my circuit, teaching and inquiring of God as I go. But you, my dear friends, I will most surely accommodate. This year I will skip the north."

"That's right. That's right," Naomi encouraged him.

Elimelech stood speechless. This wagon had started downhill and was gathering speed.

"And for my husband's generosity you will return with full payment plus a tithe."

"Full payment plus a tithe in silver."

Naomi rose up and reached for Elimelech's hand. "See how we'll improve *our* fortunes in the end?"

ELIMELECH, COME UP HERE! A girl wants good news.

The heat had gone off the teapot. The winter's day was darkening. Inside the upper room the women enjoyed a cozy homeliness. But outside—as unlikely as this is in Bethlehem—the air carried the snap of snow.

Elimelech tromped up the stairs and in the door.

Naomi knew how like briars were her thousand

wrinkles. At the same time she knew how handsomely her cheekbones had framed her Judean face. As soon as he entered, she wrapped her arms around him and tilted her head and lifted a well-scented charm to Elimelech's ear. In a low, warm breath she whispered, "Come. Share joy with our daughter. Take pleasure in her pleasure." She hummed a musical note of promise. "Tell Milcah about your negotiations with her father. Tell her how successful you were in the end. *You* say it, Elimelech. Tell her that she shall marry a week from today."

10

Fighting and Nightfall

NEITHER DOES ISRAEL PREVAIL ON THE SECOND DAY of the war
with Benjamin.

Though she never gets close enough to see the combat,
Naomi can hear the bloody bellowings and interpret its
progress. All day she labors among the wagons, ministering
to those who were wounded yesterday.

She cleans dirt and pus from festering wounds, cools
infections with an extract of grape seed. She treats burns
with garlic. She sets bones by wrapping sections of spear-
shafts tight against a leg or an arm. She shaves away the
day-old scabbing, cuts ragged flesh to smooth its edges,
disinfects the gash, and stitches it together. She bleeds
or cauterizes, then bandages puncture wounds—flight
of arrows, thrust of javelins. Naomi utters prayers over
the hopeless, tranquilizes the terrified, sends those who
can walk for water, instructs the weak to bury the dead.
"Now!" she commands. "Do it before the sun sets."

And all the while she interprets to the sounds of the

fighting, brothers on brothers, tribes and peoples of the same God.

Choppy sounds, roarings fractured in ten thousand pieces, howls, grunts, cursings, shouts of bloody triumphs, bits of psalms shrieked to heaven, again and again the name of the Lord. Cracks of the captain's commands.

Often the sheer intensity of hand-to-hand combat subdues the human voices. Then the clashings of metal weapons define the battleground; shields grinding together, the *thunk* of battleaxes, hoofbeats and feet pounding the ground in retreat. Glory has gone out of the air.

The warriors are returning. In the distance Naomi hears jubilant voices, Benjamin marching home again.

But the armies of Israel stumble back to the wagons and drive the wagons back to their degenerating camps.

Naomi never stops working. Straightway she turns from yesterday's wounds to tend to those of today.

She established her nursing station in Salmon's tent, which is in the center of the armies of Israel. Salmon arrives, dismounts, and stands in the door-flap. The healer is winding a bandage around the face of a soldier who lost his nose. Without raising her head she charges Salmon with a task.

"Send ten throughout the camps. Tell them to bring the worst of the wounded here. Find ten others with steady hands and patience. I'll show them how to treat the simpler cases."

Many soldiers have fallen, and many close to despair, and what can a woman do to encourage their spirits? Even the chiefs don't walk upright. They maunder.

Naomi is of two minds. To the degree that she loves Milcah—raped and murdered less than a week ago—even to that same degree she craves the execution of Gibeah. Israel *must* strike with a heavenly vengeance.

On the other hand, Israel is tearing itself apart. It is one family, one land, one father Jacob—*twelve* the number God ordained, but the twelve are destroying themselves. Naomi grew up with the daughters of Rosh, who was a *Benjamite*.

Evening spreads its blue-black blanket over the tents of Israel, down the hillside and over the valleys. The blanket muffles the voices of men, their groanings, their sobbings, their pain.

The chiefs shuffle together. They go up to the sanctuary and fall before the Ark of the Lord and wail again, the third night in a row.

For the chiefs, for ten thousand campfires speckling the black earth, Naomi sings:

> *You are known in Judah, O God!*
> *Your name is great in Israel.*
> *Your mercy sits among us*
> *on the Ark in the shrine at Bethel.*
> *O break the flashing arrows!*
> *Shatter the shields,*
> *snap the swords,*
> *the weapons of our enemies!*

Israel's armies close their mouths.

It is the Hakamah, they think. *It is Naomi.* Bethlehem

is moved by the familiar voice, and the night becomes a comfort.

> *Glorious are you, more majestic*
> *than the everlasting mountains.*
> *Stout Gibeah shall be stripped of his spoil*
> *and sink into a solemn sleep.*
> *At your rebuke, O God of Jacob,*
> *let rider and horse lie stunned....*

"Mama?"

Naomi looks and sees in poor torchlight a young man, his arm slung over his father's neck, a strong man bearing him hither.

Mahlon and Elimelech! Mahlon's left thigh has been slashed from the hip to the knee. Gouts of drying blood cover the leg like a sleeve. He's awake, but barely. His feet turn inward. He would collapse except for his father.

Naomi murmurs, "Elimelech."

The man says, "Naomi."

Eighteen thousand men have fallen today.

The chiefs strike their foreheads against the ground and wail and wail. All day long they have fasted. But to no avail.

Now, for an atonement on their behalf, Phinehas offers the Lord a lamb. He burns the creature whole, sending its smoke to the Most High God.

Phinehas follows this with a second offering, this to beg peace between the children and their Lord. Only the fat of this beast is burned. The chiefs wash their hands and break their fast by eating its meat.

Finally they sit in a hushed mortification before the Ark while Phinehas inquires of the Lord what he wants of Israel tomorrow.

"Shall we again battle against our brethren the Benjamites, or shall we cease?"

The Lord says, *Go up. For tomorrow I will give them into your hand.*

Naomi sits in Salmon's tent. Her son sleeps, his head on her lap. She rocks him and sings, "Into thy hand I commit my spirit."

Even now she will not cry. Even now she neither mourns nor rejoices.

The night is far gone. The injured have ceased coming. They have all lain down.

Elimelech and Salmon are huddling in a high cavern with all the captains of Israel, developing tactics for the third assault not more than four hours away.

For tomorrow I will give them into your hand.

Except Naomi, no one has cared for Milcah more than Mahlon. It was Mahlon who lay across the gameboard from his adopted sister, winning, losing, both of them in childhood sharpening their minds. He knew of her bruises. He worried for her health. It was Mahlon who put the puzzle directly to his mother. When he was no older than nine years, he asked: "If Milcah's father beats her, why does she keep … I don't know … keep making up to him?"

His question sparked her sudden illumination.

"Because she fears him." Mahlon's confusion had been her own. Now she understood: "Because she thinks that love and obedience will finally persuade him that she is a good girl."

They both felt sad that goodness could be so confused by evil.

It was Mahlon, the older brother, who wept in the morning before the war.

And when Milcah crept back to Bethlehem suffering the guilt of a murderess, it was Mahlon who walked beside her in the orchards.

No other man — not one of the men who knew her during her lifetime — wept for the death of Milcah but Mahlon.

Naomi's son sleeps fitfully. His head twists in her lap. Periodically a limb will jerk as if in a dream. But with all her might Naomi holds his left leg still, or else he could rip his stitches and lose more blood than his poor, pale body has left to offer.

Hush, the night and the dewfall. Be still, O foreign winds, you winds that blow from the east. O Lord God, spread your wings over my son, and the hem of your garment over his soul. For he lies between light and the darkness of the trench, between the living and the dead.

11

When Milcah of the
White Hands Married

A WOMAN MARRIES ON WEDNESDAY. Everyone knows that she is a virgin, if she marries on a Wednesday.

Milcah stood naked in a great basin of warm water. The water was scented. So was the oil with which Naomi massaged her ivory-white skin.

The Women of Bethlehem were burning an aromatic treebark in Elimelech's courtyard. To drive away unhealthy spirits, they fanned the smoke into the room and over the body of the bride. They wove her wreath of myrtle leaves. They hung chains of fruit all around the sides of the cart soon to carry her through the village to her husband. They hung evergreen boughs from the bench upon which she would sit.

Naomi combed Milcah's wet hair and twisted it and oiled it into a deep sheen, and then stood back to marvel at the column of grace before her.

"You are beautiful. You are beautiful."

She offered her daughter a hand and helped her to step

from the basin onto a pretty little dais Elimelech had built for the bride's white feet.

Naomi set a pot of liquid henna on the shelf by her elbow. She dipped the fine hairs of a brush into the dye, then with unerring strokes drew designs on skin as smooth as vellum: whorls on the backs of Milcah's hands; arabesques up her arms and shoulders and forehead and cheeks; scrolling lines of the red-brown dye between her breasts and down her stomach even to the closing of her thighs, surprises for her husband in the lamplight. Naomi enlarged her daughter's eyes with charcoal above and below her lashes and lines drawn back to each of her temples.

"You are beautiful."

The women came forward and dressed Milcah in a supple tunic, over which they draped a robe of shining fleece. And upon her bosom, a necklace of agate stones.

Naomi stepped to the door of the courtyard.

"Elimelech." Milcah's mother radiated gladness. "Come get the daughter worth twenty fields and all the hills of Judah."

Elimelech and his sons came and made a cradle of their arms and carried their sister out to the cart.

Milcah, sunlight blazing in her beautiful hair—Milcah kept her head bowed as if everyone were expecting someone else. Surely such affection must be a mistake. Why would women walk the winding streets beside her cart, ululating a festival joy?

Truth be told, Milcah was looking backward more than forward. It was Naomi who filled her heart, and Naomi's precious family, and the use the village had found for her. The peasants were as ready to receive her healings as Naomi's.

Oh, my friends, I am not worthy.

Bethlehem behind her. And ahead of her ... was an unfolded road. What sort of man was this Levite after all? He spoke in exotic accents, wonderful but strange. And two wives. What would that mean?

Nevertheless, Milcah smiled and permitted herself a glance at the people dancing around her, a procession on *her* account, a day given over to her alone! What Milcah saw caused her more pleasure than she could ever deserve.

One cloud dampened the day, but not the bride's heart. Milcah rode her cart completely unaware of the fool behind. Great boo-hooings moistened the morning: Ezra the tanner bewailing his daughter.

The Women of Bethlehem spent the day in love and loss.

Goodbye, gentle Milcah! Goodbye, Milcah of the white hands.

God be with you, child of Bethlehem.

And so the Levite and his wife traveled north into the hills of Ephraim on two donkeys, and a servant went with them to see to their needs.

Naomi smiled. It seemed pure and appropriate that the almond trees had just today begun to wake from the winter's sleep, their leafless branches bursting into wedding-white flowers.

12

Four Months and Four Months, and Mere Days Before the War

FOUR MONTHS LATER MILCAH CREPT BACK TO BETHLEHEM, ashamed, moving through the night to hide in Elimelech's house and to weep in Naomi's embrace.

"Daughter. What's the matter?"

To Milcah's humiliation, the story was common, no different from the rest of her life. Except that she brought back a soul burning with coals of a violent sin.

Milcah, fifteen years old, and a babe in arms again.

WHEN THE LEVITE WAS HOME, he spent his energies and attentions and his money and all his sexual prowess upon his second wife. Milcah never questioned his behavior, for this was precisely the life he had promised her. It was the best she knew of marriage. He dressed her well and gave her gifts and called her body "his pearl" and "lily of the lily-seed."

Nevertheless, she lived unsatisfied. Every night she begged God to remove the pride that was thirstier than the cups of kings. What *did* she want? Nothing. She couldn't imagine anything that might improve her husband's attentions. Hadn't she yearned with all her heart to escape her father's cruelties? Yes, and this husband never so much as raised his voice to her.

But Milcah had grown up watching Naomi and Elimelech. And though she never considered her life to be like theirs, she hungered for the devotion they shared, yet she was unaware of the spirit possessing her heart.

Milcah had schooled herself in contentment before. Surely she could live here not unhappily.

But the Levite traveled. Torah was his tool, and inquiring of the Lord his commodity. Wherever he went he filled his scrip with the gifts of the faithful. Even so did he provide lavishly for his household. But he took both donkeys with him.

The wives were denied the strength of animal labor.

Lacking a servant that followed his master, and borne down by her own mountainous fat, the first wife forced the second to serve in the servant's place. It didn't occur to Milcah to complain. She accepted the greater work as the natural duty of a second, stronger, younger wife.

But during the first three months of the marriage, the older wife's contempt for Milcah increased to loathing and then to hatred.

Immediately after the Levite left on a trip, within minutes of his departure, the woman seemed to swell, to beat black wings inside the house, her head growing as red and raw as a vulture's.

"He don't love you! Y' think you *know* that hog, you whore? Think he treasures you? Well, y'ain't climbed no ladder over me! You're his piss-purse. You're the puddle o' blood for his pitiful seed, is all. Watch! *Watch!* He'll light out on you same's he did on me. Wait and see if he don't."

Milcah strove never to answer her tirades — not until the end, and then just once.

At first it was a matter of humble obedience. Milcah refused to acknowledge the storms breaking over her. She kept working as if in her own little cubby. But what seemed like disdain caused the first wife to spit bile. She demanded that Milcah turn and pay attention. Milcah paid attention, but with her head bowed down. The woman shrieked orders that Milcah *look* at her; that Milcah must show some grit and *answer* her.

"Fight me, white worm! Lick-spittle dog, get up and *fight* with me!"

It was Milcah's passivity that drove the woman mad. Fury extended her fingers like a hawk's talons. In spite of her weight she flew at Milcah and raked her white chest bloody.

(Naomi: Oh, child, let me see.

Milcah raised the tunic to her neck.

Naomi growled.)

Finally, in the middle of a spring night Milcah woke up sweating and gasping for a breath. An enormous pressure was squashing the air from her lungs. The enormous woman-wife sat astride her, brooches in both fists, the long needles like spines between her fingers.

"Uglify my pretty lily!" she hissed. "Slash the petals in her cheeks!"

What Milcah did next she did in a flash.

She doubled her torso upward so suddenly the witch slewed sideways. Both women scrambled to stand, but Milcah was faster. In a single, circular motion she caught up a ladle from its hook, swung it over her head and brought it down like a hammer on the Levite's first wife's skull.

That woman dropped like a sack full of grain and lay still.

THE WHEAT FIELDS BOWED WAVE UPON WAVE in the vagrant late-spring breezes. They were changing their clothes from green to gold, preparing for the reapers soon to come.

Barley had just been harvested. Elimelech sent Milcah outside the gate to work on the threshing floors. When the wind was up, villagers used their long winnowing forks to toss the barley into the air, separating the heavier grain from the straw, and the straw from the chaff.

Milcah wanted to hide her face from Bethlehem. She was a criminal more guilty than those who had danced at her wedding could imagine.

But Elimelech would have none of this. If she showed up in public there was bound to be gossip. But if she *didn't* show up, the gossip would grow since even good people seek drama in their humdrum lives. Both Elimelech and Naomi believed that Milcah's humble manner and her steadfast industry (and the sadness of her countenance) would move Bethlehem to tenderness. As for those who insisted on reproaching her, well, Elimelech's trust in the child and Naomi's authority in Bethlehem would eventually shut their mouths.

AFTER FOUR MORE MONTHS HAD PASSED, Milcah was a child of the village again. A whiff of mystery still followed her, but that curled the toes of the more romantic.

It was Mahlon's presence that had drawn the sting from Milcah's soul. They didn't talk much. Sitting together worked. Playing board games without conversation, without a need for scoring or even the need to end a game — that worked. The more she accepted Mahlon's brothering, the more freely she went out in Bethlehem.

Peace, Milcah of the white hands. You are home again.

And then came the grape harvest, and the bubbling laughter of those who stepped into the wide stone vats, and tucked their skirts up under their sashes, and treaded the juice from the grapes.

They danced. Inside the vats and outside on dry grasses, their feet empurpled and their hearts carefree, the women danced. They sang songs of simple hilarity, songs of lovers transported, and songs of lovers down and raunchy.

Naomi accompanied the celebrations by strumming her harp at exhilarating speeds.

Sunburned faces grinned. Women and men threw back their heads, brown teeth showing, laughing themselves breathless. This year, *this* year the Lord has spilled his bounty upon us.

And Milcah trod the grapes as well — more quietly, this

songless thrush, but smiling for the happiness like rain around her. Milcah expressed her own cheer with colors. She bound up the masses of her hair in a scarf of yellow and red—yellow from a walnut dye and red from the roots of the madder herb.

It was Mahlon who first saw that Milcah was standing as still as marble in the midst of the jubilation. She was staring north. He followed her sightline and recognized the Levite riding on one of two donkeys grandly unto Bethlehem.

Suddenly Milcah broke and sprinted through the city gates.

Mahlon ran after her. She disappeared into his father's house, quick as a wren into her nest. He found his poor sister crouched between two rolled-up pallets, covering her face and quivering. She was hissing a prayer—a prayer that she should die. In an instant the past four months had vanished.

Mahlon reached, but she shrank from his touch.

Bare feet are not sandals. Sandals make noise. The sole of a woman's foot need not announce its coming.

Something like a sound-shadow passed over Mahlon and then over Milcah. His mother, Naomi. He withdrew.

"Milcah? Why are you hiding here?"

At the sound of her mother's voice, the poor child went to pieces. Such a wailing poured out of Elimelech's house, that silence descended on the Women of Bethlehem.

Surely judgment was about to crash through the clouds and blot out her wretched life.

The Levite said to Naomi, "I know my fault. It is the fault of none but me."

"Your fault," she said. "Then why have you come to accuse your wife?"

"Oh, no! She's clean. There is no stain upon the lovely Milcah."

The Levite was kneeling at Naomi's feet. "Milcah is innocent. How could I ever accuse my lily?"

"Then make your confession, Levite. What *is* your fault?"

"Please, let me arise and go in. I have no heart until I see her again."

"Levite! *Tell me your fault!*"

With a steadfast glare, Naomi was fixing the perfumed fellow to the ground. Her silence forced him out of smiles and circumlocutions.

"Well. Ah. I neglected Milcah, my second wife—her. But I love her. I am most devoted to her. Mother, I desire to prove it by taking her once more into my household."

"You neglected her. What does that mean?"

The Levite folded his hands and lifted them. The strain of his uncharacteristic posture and the flat, white heat of the day had darkened his armpits with sweat.

"I neglected her. I mean, I didn't know. I wasn't aware ..."

"Out with it, man!"

"When traveling, you see, I wasn't aware how my first wife served my second."

What *is* this? It's easy enough for priests to denounce sinners. It's their delight!

"The head of his household," Naomi said, "*blind* to his household?"

"I'm sorry. I'm sorry. It was only when I came home and found one wife weeping on account of a bump on her head, and the other gone—"

"The woman isn't dead?"

"What? Dead? No!"

The shift in Naomi's mood must have looked to the Levite like acceptance. He puffed and pushed and got back to his feet.

Her angry interrogation turned into gleeful interrogation.

"And you waited a full four months before you came to ease her soul and to swear your love for my daughter? Four months?"

"But that particular transgression is not mine, mother Naomi. It seemed proper to divorce the first wife first. I was considering my tender Milcah's comfort, who deserves to come home to a house entirely hers."

"It takes less than a week to get an approval for bills of divorce."

The Levite paused. "But there was the matter of cause, you see. That woman … was incapable of adultery."

"Is it nothing to you that she ripped the skin of my daughter's, your wife's, chest? 'That woman' scored eight scars across her 'tenderness.' Isn't that cause enough?"

The Levite bowed his face, quick tears filling his eyes. "I didn't know. Word of the Lord, I didn't know!"

One more time Naomi brewed her sage tea and asked Milcah to join her upstairs. They sat down in the cool of the evening. The older woman put her forefinger to

Milcah's lips, and gazed into the younger woman's eyes, searching the heart.

"Do you remember the day I found you in the cave? And helped you carry your water jar home?"

Milcah nodded.

"Do you remember when I anointed your eyes and healed the infection that was blinding you?"

A silent nod.

"Milcah. I am the same woman as I was then. And I love you no less than I loved you then. Oh, my daughter, how I yearn to heal you all over again."

Naomi drew back from her daughter, trying to hide her sudden rush of emotion. She turned her eyes toward the ridge in the west, and willed the tears away.

When she began to speak, it was in stronger measures.

"You don't know this, but your blood-father has been trying to assert his authority over you again. If you belong to no husband, he says, you belong to him, that dog's pizzle! He has accosted Elimelech for two months now. Elimelech refuses to pay attention. So now the tanner has brought his case to the elders in the gate.

"Milcah, you *must* pay attention to the Levite. You must know that the law supports your father's claim. Therefore Bethlehem, as much as it loves you, is about to make you a slave, child! A more terrible slavery than you've ever known. Go to Ephraim. Go with the Levite and be free."

Milcah began to shake. Her shoulders hunched as if she were expecting a beating.

"No!" Naomi's word cracked like a rebuke. "I know what you think. I should've said this right away. No, child, there was no murder! And for everything else, *everything* else, the Levite accepts the blame."

Suddenly Naomi heard the harshness of her tone. It must have sounded like a scolding, but it came of her own fear that Milcah might reject the Levite. Naomi glanced at the young woman sitting beside her, and was moved by the tenderness there, and by the color of her skin, rouged under the sunset sky.

Naomi crooked a finger under Milcah's chin and lifted the lovely face to her own. "Truly, Milcah. There was no iniquity. You are not guilty. It has been unnecessary sorrow. You knocked the woman out, but *only* out and not to death. Look at me. Milcah? Look at me."

Sunshine and black clouds and rainbows between them: the girl's face was an uncertain atmosphere. Lingering sin? Relief? Release?

Naomi said, "Choose the Levite. Set yourself free from the misery here. You are already free from the torments in Ephraim. You shall be his only wife. This is the truth. The mistress of your own house. You will bring value to Ephraim—and Ephraim will be grateful for a midwife and a healer. Hush, hush, and a Hakamah hereafter."

Milcah said, "He has no fields."

That she had spoken at all was more important to Naomi than what she'd said.

"How can we let that stand in the way of your happiness?"

13

The Precipitating Event

THE STORY WHICH THE LEVITE TOLD ISRAEL AT MIZPAH was not the whole of the story.

There is another witness to Milcah's rape. It is the Levite's servant who now brings the truer testimony to light after his master has wandered away from the camps, drowning in despair.

Ezra whined to get his daughter back, but he was not as destitute as when he was a tanner. Eight months ago he had taken possession of Elimelech's field. Simply, it was his nature to grab whatever he could get.

In fact, his harvest had been as rich as everyone else's. And he congratulated himself on the bargain that would keep enriching him for years to come. He hired stoneworkers to lay a foundation for a new house. A house as respectable as Elimelech's, and built inside the city walls!

It was the first day of Sukkoth, the festival of harvest home, wine-making *and* wine-drinking, yes! And the Man of God had returned. And where should so glorious a sojourner celebrate if not with his father-in-law? Yes!

Truth be told, Ezra didn't really have a house. Not yet. So he commanded peasants to construct an excellent booth on his impressive properties.

And the Levite, not particularly loving the man, but loving the flow of wealth and an endless wineskin, accepted.

He was already packed. He planned to leave at noon, the first day of the In-Gathering. But the wine delighted his brains, and rich meats his stomach, so that he was genuinely surprised to discover that the day had turned into night.

The following morning a headache persuaded the Levite to stay a while longer—and so the pattern was established: midnight drinkings caused morning hangovers which begged another midnight of drinking, and a Levite grew to love a tanner.

On the fifth day, early in the afternoon, the master of his servant heaved himself to his feet.

"God knows how I praise a good man's hospitality," he said—but stubbed the tip of his Anatolian slipper on a stone and split the seam of it. Out popped his great toe, like a slug come up to look around. Both men burst into a boozy laughter.

"Hoo-hoo," the great man said, straightening his back. "It's late, my friend. We *have* to go."

Ezra, the father-in-law, nearly in tears, threw open his arms and cried, "I love you, my only-est friend in the world."

And the Levite, weeping, fell into the skinny embrace, and they both went down.

In fondness and deep fellowship, the son-in-law worked

the armlet down his fat flesh and slipped it up the limb of the tanner. What a by-God, beautiful friendship.

So, thoroughly flushed and filled with confidence, the Levite called for his donkeys and his baggage and his wife, and left Bethlehem full of song.

When darkness snaked out from the forests, the Levite's servant pulled out a stone-club and watched for wolves or bears.

Off to his right, houses in silhouette upon a high hill, he saw Jebus, a city of foreigners, Canaanites.

"Master, it's getting dark. I think we should spend the night in Jebus."

The Levite interrupted his song. "Why?" The word floated up from well-moistened lips.

"If it isn't beasts, it's thieves," said the servant. "We need safety."

"But *Jebus*, boy! You can't trust a pagan."

So the Levite and his wife kept riding, and the servant walked with a bridle and a club.

Later, both the master and his servant saw the fires of Gibeah.

"Here, now," the Levite said. "Sons of Benjamin! God-fearers." It never occurred to him to ask the opinion of a wife. He kicked his donkey, and hers followed his into Gibeah.

Like Bethlehem, Gibeah's city square was just inside the gates. The servant spread a cloak across a stone bench whereon his master nestled his butt. Of his own accord the servant helped Milcah down from her mount and led her to a seat beside the master.

The Levite folded his arms, saying, "Some citizen will honor us with a dry room and food the night."

Benjamites passed by, indeed. But so did the time. Every time his master's wife pulled her robe more tightly around herself, the servant worried.

The Levite had a headache. He lifted his orotund voice to recite Torah. What could be so base as to pass a man who knew Torah by heart?

Finally an old man carrying three dead birds and a torch cocked an ear toward the Levite. He walked over and brought the flame close to the big man's face.

"By God," he said, "I think I see an Ephraimite."

The Levite peered back. "I am an Ephraimite. By your accent, you're one too."

Well, well, sons of the same country. The Levite recognized the hand of God, accepting the old man's invitation without a second thought. "What is the trouble with Gibeah? Why won't Benjamites give a sanctified man a bed and shelter for a night?"

But his criticism was swallowed up in fumosity, for this was the last night of Sukkoth, and wine puts away unspirited talk.

The servant fed and groomed the beasts, laid out a pallet for his silent mistress, brought her bread and water, and sat himself in a far corner.

Soon the countrymen were howling mordant melodies.

Too loud and too self-satisfied, they didn't hear the pounding on the outside door.

It was the servant's heart that ran cold. The pounding

increased. Godawful voices started roaring in the street. It must have been a score of men.

BOOM!

That was a sledge. Or a battering ram against the old man's outer door.

Song fled from the besotted Ephraimites. Their eyes grew round as millstones.

The servant was panting. What was his duty now? He was a boy, not a warrior. His mistress was sitting up with her arms wrapped around her knees.

Rocks shattered the lattices.

"Send out the fat one!" *A score* of men? As far as the servant was concerned, it was an army—guttural, hoarse, lascivious: "Send out that pink hog, old man, and we won't burn ya stinking house down!"

The host jumped up and doused the torch and stomped on the coals and the room fell dark. The Levite's teeth were chattering. "O God, O God, O God, I love thee, I adore thee ..."

A flaming spear pierced the floor of the courtyard.

"Come out, cream bitch! I gotta urge! Hoo-weee, I'm a whip and a hot jack-spout."

It was the servant who dashed out with a blanket and snuffed the flame of the spear. There was dry straw in the donkey stalls.

The old Ephraimite covered his ears and shrieked, "The man's a guest! This man is a guest! A *Levite!* How could you even *think* such vile things?"

The Levite sat stark-frozen in horror.

A howl of sexual heat rose over the wall: "Your guest's our goat for the rutting!"

Two flaming arrows hissed down, one biting a wooden post, the other clattering against a plastered wall. The host screamed, "Take my daughter! Take his wife!"

A torch came looping over the wall, and another, and these were more than the servant could handle—and suddenly his master was in motion. He grabbed his wife's arm and dragged her through the courtyard to the doorway. He kicked the door open and threw Milcah out and slammed the door again and fell to the ground with his back against its wood, panting and panting, a very fat man.

The servant saw this in a fast glance while squirting skins and skins of water over the fires, dousing them and quenching light in the house. All light. They could hear beasts snarling outside. The servant despised himself. No one moved until the morning.

In the quietness of a new dawn, the Levite roused himself, cursed the lack of water, and commanded the servant to pack and to bridle the donkeys.

When he opened the courtyard door, there lay Milcah face down in the dust, her right hand clutching the threshold at the toes of her husband's Anatolian slippers.

"Get up," he said. He stepped over her. "Get up. We're going."

She didn't answer. So he lifted the woman and slung her belly-down over the saddle of his second donkey.

After traveling high hills, one behind the other, and arriving home in the afternoon, he saw that his wife was dead.

So he took a knife and laying hold of her body, hacked her limb from limb into twelve separate pieces, which he sent to the tribes of Israel, saying, "Such a thing has never happened from the day we came out of Egypt until this day."

14

"If You Go, I Will Sew Myself Closed against Your Lusts!"

WELL BEFORE DAWN, THE THIRD DAY OF THE WAR, a small contingent of Israelites slips into the brush surrounding Gibeah. They conceal themselves as surely as leopards lie in wait.

Ram's horns sound outside of the camps of Israel, down and down a long front until Salmon blows the eleventh horn. Judah roars and shudders the earth with a thousand feet running. As the armies charge past him, Salmon restrains his white donkey. She dances and spins in the excitement but doesn't follow. Boaz tears south, the first of the battle line, the point of the spear of the lion of Judah. He wears the helmet and the coat of mail. Elimelech keeps pace farther back among his brother bowmen.

All the armies of Israel pour toward Gibeah exactly as they've done twice before. Salmon kicks his mount up a stony ridge. So do the other captains, stationing themselves like towers east and farther east of Salmon. Everything—every action, every cry, every flourish, every manner of

109

attack—repeats the actions of the two days preceding. And Benjamin stands fast like a cliff against which the rolling breaker crashes and collapses.

Within three hours Israel is failing.

Salmon puts the ram's horn to his lips and—like the angel whose shout stopped the sun for Joshua—blows a shrill *Retreat!*

The warriors need no second command. All of them, all the fighting Israelites reel around and set their faces to the rear.

Benjamin laughs in the might of his right arm. Oh, with what glories he has clothed himself!

But of course! How else could the day go? The third defeat will be a complete defeat. Israel is humiliated, eleven tribes repulsed by one, their armies racing for home.

Rise up, O Benjamin! Charge after the rest, capture Israel and rule him altogether!

The last Israelite in retreat is Boaz ben-Salmon. His expression is a churn of powerful emotions, for there is majesty in the cast of his head, but in his glittering eye, mortification. He lingers dead-still on his left foot as if he were leveling a scornful dare at his enemies. But then he too turns and bounds like an antelope over the gorse and thickets.

But between each flight, he dallies. Boaz is calculating speeds and distances, keeping himself just outside the reach of the enemy's arrows and stones. Swiftly to the left, then the right, his quiver looped over the shoulder, dagger and sword clasped in his girdle, and in his hands a bow and a spear. Boaz bristles with weapons. In fact, under the guise of a dodging retreat, Boaz is playing a waiting game. The last to leave the field, he intends to be first returning. He lifts his eyes to the horizon. It's there he'll see the sign for—

And then a black smoke rolls up the southern sky.

Boaz roars, "It's *our* fight now! O bloody Benjamin—turn back and behold your own destruction!"

The mad glee of that single warrior halts several of his enemies. They glance rearward, and cry out in dismay. Others break stride and turn. The entire battle line falters. Boaz draws his curved sword and slices the neck of the nearest soldier. He guts a second, cracks the skull of a third. Benjamin loses heart. Now the great wave of Israelites has changed course, looming higher and higher over Benjamin's seven hundred. None of them can hold his ground. They lunge away. They scatter and fly like quail.

For Gibeah is in flames! As soon as the village was left unguarded, Israelites jumped from their hiding places, dashed through the gates, and set fire to every hut and house. Benjamin watches black smoke boil upward, and runs off to the east.

Judah, Reuben, Dan—*all* the force of the eleven tribes, bright with vengeance, give chase, slaughtering those who slip and stumble, driving the faster soldiers forward, biting into the muscle-meat of the fleeing troops.

While arrows decimate their numbers, five thousand falling before the sword, troops and women and children and the aged and cattle and sheep and Benjamin's villages are slaughtered. Strings of listless smoke wander upward from the ashes.

Before the sun sets, the entire tribe of Benjamin has

been reduced to six hundred, men who have blockaded themselves in a stronghold at the rock of Rimmon.

Several chiefs suggest a siege. This is a wilderness of no food and little water.

But suddenly the hearts of the Israelites melt. The thought of starving the last remnant of the twelfth tribe horrifies them.

What have we done?

And even if Israel does *not* blot these six hundred from the Book of Life, how will they produce offspring without women or wives to bear a next generation? No, there is not one Eve left alive to deliver one child for the saving of a dying tribe.

The chiefs, their captains, and their troops march back to Bethel in order to seek some solution.

"We swore an oath," they remind each other. "When we first gathered at Mizpah and Benjamin was our enemy, we swore never to give our daughters as wives to him."

It seemed an appropriate punishment then. *Rape just one of our women and all of our women are withheld from you forever.*

So now Israel sits one more time before the Ark of the Lord, weeping bitterly.

"O Lord, the God of Israel, why has this come to pass that there should be today one tribe lacking?"

IN THE MORNING THE CHIEFS RISE EARLY and build an altar and offer burnt offerings and peace offerings. They discuss the sad matter among themselves. "What shall we do for wives for those who are left?"

Elimelech and Naomi and Mahlon sit in earshot. Though Naomi can muster some pity for the desolations of Benjamin, and though she understands that the loss of one brother could chop the others into eleven pieces, their question agitates her. The very frame of the question feels wrong. Naomi will not commit herself to Israel until she knows Israel's solution.

She glances at her husband. He's listening intently, his lips pursed, missing nothing. She can't find skepticism in his face. Why does *that* trouble her?

But maybe Elimelech only wants to make an accurate record of the proceedings for the sake of his cousin Salmon. Neither Naomi nor Elimelech had seen Salmon on his white donkey after yesterday's victory. Again this morning her husband trotted through the camps without success. Not Salmon, not Boaz either.

"When we first arrived at Mizpah," the chiefs say, "when we swore our oath," they say, "was there *anyone* who wasn't with us then?"

"Well, yes." A chief of Manasseh stands up. "Jabesh-gilead. When we mustered all Manasseh to march against Benjamin, Jabesh-gilead ignored the call."

So: there was one city who swore no oath.

The chiefs and the captains deliver themselves of their solution: "Send twelve thousand of our bravest across the Jordan to Jabesh-gilead. Command them to kill with the edges of their sword every inhabitant, men and women and children. Except! Let no one dispatch a virgin! Let no man take a virgin for himself!"

Naomi cries out, "In God's name, *Israel!*"

The headmen continue, heedless of a single voice of protest: "These are the virgins our brothers will go into, and Benjamin shall live."

Naomi is on her feet. "For the rape of one you'll rape six hundred? And you think you're righteous?" She wants a tongue of lightning. She throws herself into a run—but the hand of her husband stops her. She strikes at him, screaming, "Who will the Women of Bethlehem bewail now? There aren't sisters enough. Elimelech! There aren't *eyes* enough to weep for the maidens of Jabesh-gilead—"

"Naomi! Hold your tongue."

"If you go, Elimelech, by *God* I will sew myself shut against your lusts!"

Her son stands up on a splint and a staff. "Mother!"

Elimelech wraps his arms around his wife and holds her mightily. She recognizes wisdom and affection, and she sees that his face has gone white, the tip of his nose bloodless.

He murmurs, "I choose life."

His word is a witness, and the spirit of Moses moves between them:

> *I call heaven and earth to witness against*
> *you this day,*
> *that I have set before you life and death,*
> *blessing and cursing.*
> *Therefore choose life,*
> *that your descendants may live.*

AS SLOWLY AS A FUNERAL MARCH, Naomi and Elimelech walk back to Bethlehem. Naomi limps. Mahlon's leg is so tightly encased in bandages that it is as stiff as a post. The war cut his muscle through and through. He leans on a hasty crutch.

There is no ox. There is no wagon. Elimelech carries the tent and their weapons on his back. Mahlon has tied several skins of water to his belt "to keep me balanced."

About midmorning they cross into the northern portion of Benjamin, and enter the land that Naomi cursed five days ago. This is a dead land, deserted, stinking of blood and soot. The force of her curse now wrings her soul with guilt.

> *Let their days be few.*
> *Let their sons be driven*
> *from a city destroyed ...*

These were the words. These were the sentiments she uttered in hatred.

> *Cut them off from the earth, O Lord!*
> *Blot out their names by the second generation ...*

But now who deserves greater blame than Naomi herself? Behold the devastations of her wrath. Empty out your bag of medicines, Hakamah! Roll boulders into it. Carry on your back the curses that have laid waste the land the Lord promised—

"Naomi," Elimelech says. "Look!" He jogs off to the right.

Mahlon breathes, "Oh no."

Naomi can see two figures below a fall of stone, but barely. As she limps the tableau becomes clearer. One man crouches stiff as stone beside another man. That one is stretched flat on his back. "Salmon!" A white donkey stands patiently behind them. Naomi yells, "Boaz?" Yes! But the son is holding his father's head in a grip of iron — himself rigid and immobilized.

Elimelech is already kneeling by Boaz.

But Salmon's hair is thick with coagulating blood. His helmet has fallen nearby, the rawhide crushed, a violent arrow thrust halfway through the side of it.

Naomi looks at Elimelech. "I asked," he says. "Boaz isn't answering."

A ragged shirt of mail has been bunched under Salmon's neck. Naomi kneels beside her husband.

"Boaz? It's your aunt Naomi." The man's face is streaked as if by whip-wounds. His breathing is inaudible, his expression closed against heaven and earth.

Salmon's eye sockets are covered in a scabrous blood as if by copper coins. The muscles in his face are slack, his lips open upon a crescent, his breath foul. But there *is* a breath. Naomi works her fingers through his hair.

Elimelech says, "No need to ask why they didn't return to camp last night." He closes his broad hands around the son's forearms and gently forces them away from his father's skull. A viscous red plug appears on Boaz's palm.

Naomi says, "My knife."

Mahlon finds it and hands it over. She shaves a bald patch on the side of Salmon's head and studies the puncture wound. Tenderly she explores the head on opposite sides, and around and around, then leans back.

"He was shot in the head. There's a fine crack through the skull bone. Boaz must have pulled the arrow out." She points to a soft, moist tissue inside the hole. "It's his brain," she says. "Swelling."

Suddenly, violently, Salmon throws his head back and begins to thrash.

Naomi falls on his body. "Elimelech!" Elimelech worms his arms around the neck of the convulsing man to hold the wound away from the dirt.

"Boaz!" Naomi cries. She slaps him hard. "Boaz! I need mandrake roots!"

She puts her forehead against Salmon's forehead and begins to shout-sing:

> *He forgives all your iniquities,*
> *heals you of your diseases,*
> *redeems your life from the Pit,*
> *crowns you with steadfast love ...*

Boaz hasn't moved. Naomi, riding Salmon's spasms, lashes the inert boy with a whip of her tongue. "There!" pointing toward the ridge. "*Those* leaves. The ones folded like a rosette. That's mandrake."

Boaz stands up and goes.

Back to Salmon, the song an eagle's shriek:

> *He satisfies you with good as long as you live,*
> *so that your youth is renewed like the eagle's—*

At his name the sick man slackens. His breathing is

reduced to tiny pumpings. Naomi signals Elimelech to release him, and she herself removes her weight. Of his own accord Mahlon has brought a skin of water which Naomi pours over Salmon's head. She washes the blood in slick lumps away. She cools his fiery flesh with wine. She bandages his whole head. She takes mandrake from Boaz and rubs the roots pliable and crushes them in a mortar, and strains the juice into a small jar of alcohol, then dribbles the medicine into the poor man's mouth.

Soon his lips smack and a long sigh indicates the easing of his mind and his body.

Naomi now looks fully at Boaz. "Take it as a good sign," she says.

In the meantime Elimelech has constructed a sturdy pallet of tent-curtains and spear-handles.

They settle the wounded man on this. Elimelech takes the wooden poles at the front of the pallet, Boaz those at the back, never removing his eyes from the face of his father. The muscle at the back of his jaw pulses. His mute intensity begins to drive the small group faster than Mahlon can go. Naomi's son falls behind. They travel the ridge road south through Benjamin, into Judah, then up the adjoining path to Bethlehem.

Not fifty paces from the gate, Salmon suddenly sits up. Boaz loses his grip. His father hits the ground and cries out, "Flames and scorpions! Shatter the alabaster! Shatter it—*now!*"

Salmon's spirit rushes from his chest in a fearful rattle. His powerful muscles clench, distorting his frame, and then there is no doubt. Fixed in this horrible posture, Salmon ben-Nahshon is dead.

Boaz backs away from the body.

Elimelech kneels beside his cousin, his friend, and kisses his face, then wraps the corpse in the stiff fabric of the tent's curtain.

Naomi whispers, "Blessed be the name of the Lord."

Mahlon closes the gap on his bandaged leg and steps toward Boaz and would touch him, but Boaz strikes the arm and knocks Mahlon down, and strides eastward through the trees until they can see him no more.

15

The Ancient Tale

IN THE DAYS WHEN THE JUDGES RULED, *there was a famine in the land, and a certain man of Bethlehem in Judah went to sojourn in the country of Moab, he and his wife and his two sons.*

The name of the man was Elimelech, and the name of his wife Naomi, and the names of his two sons were Mahlon and Chilion. They were Ephrathites from Bethlehem in Judah. They went into the country of Moab and remained there.

Part Two

BOAZ

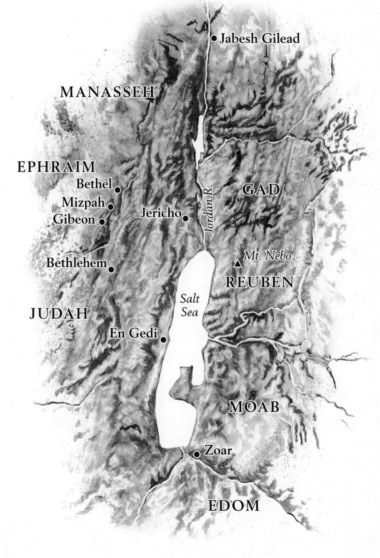

Jabesh Gilead

MANASSEH

EPHRAIM
Bethel
Mizpah
Gibeon
Jericho

Jordan R.

GAD

Bethlehem

Mt. Nebo

REUBEN

*Salt
Sea*

JUDAH

En Gedi

MOAB

Zoar

EDOM

16

Leaving Zoar

NOTHING LIVES IN THE GREAT SALT SEA. Fish that swim with the Jordan River into its waters die. Fifty miles north to south; the glut of a trench so deep no other gorge in all the earth lies deeper; bounded by massive cliffs, enclosed, imprisoned, a great body of water shut in forever—the Great Salt Sea spreads death along its shores. Gravel and marl refuse life. Green things cannot root and grow, except the terebinths and those grasses and shrubs able to swallow salt and still survive.

Sometimes the wind blasts through the funnel of its walls, increasing its speed until the heavy surface is torn into a riot of whitecaps. Otherwise, breezes blow out from the sea-canyon during the day, and during the night are sucked back into it. A stupendous serpent, breathing, sleeping.

Nevertheless, the finger of God has chosen to touch the rim of it here and there with green oases.

Several miles southeast of the southernmost point of the Salt Sea there grows an oasis lush enough to support the small town of Zoar. "Zoar," *that little thing.* A road

123

passes through the little village. It runs from the Gulf of Aqabah in the south, then connects to the King's Highway over which merchants carry their rich wares as far north as Damascus. Zoar is a resting place. Zoar benefits from an exchange of goods.

No one notices the tall, solitary man who leaves the oasis by no road at all. He wanders in a kind of distraction, slowly into the Valley of Siddim and toward the sea itself. Tar pits mark the valley floor. The man seems oblivious, gazing into the infinities—until he nearly stumbles into a pit and at the last instant pulls back.

His face has been blasted by sun and the dry air and the stinging sands. So too the skin below the nape of his neck, his arms and legs. He wears a sackcloth mantle and a loincloth. All the rest of his flesh is exposed. His beard is whitened by salt dust, his hair licked into wild loops, his eyes white in leather sockets.

The canvas pack on his back is full of the food he gathered in Zoar. He must survive on poor rations for many days to come.

Northwest, now, across the Valley of Siddim he goes. The descending sun throws his own high-stepping shadow behind him. Then the shadow vanishes. The sun is blocked by a narrow Mount Sodom, an upheaval of gypsum, shales, marl, salt. Does he see the torsos agonizing on the skirts of the mount? Can he attach to them the name of the tale Naomi told him? Does he know where he is?

The man is Boaz ben-Salmon, long-footed, his limbs rangy, his joints knobbed and awkward, his chest an empty cage of bones. But the man's spine is erect, retaining something of its old elegance.

Boaz took to the wilderness the same day his father Salmon died. Since then he hasn't ceased to roam. Ten months a pilgrim in uninhabited desolations, threading the Negev, the Wilderness of Zin, now closing in on the Great Salt Sea and walking northward.

THE PILLAR OF SALT DIRECTLY BEFORE YOU! She was a woman once. Now her person is dissolving under the infrequent rains. Her face is a wipe of sodium. There was an arm once, reaching backward. Now she is a lingering twist with neither a thought nor a mind to think it.

This was the wife of Lot, the nephew of our first father, Abraham. Abraham and Sarah traveled in tents while Lot chose to live in cities of luxury. They came to Sodom, Lot and his wife, and resided in the cool of a whitewashed house and prospered. His wife bore two daughters in that city. Fifteen years passed. The daughters grew into womanhood.

But the perversions of the men of Sodom angered Abraham's God.

The Lord sent two angels to assess the sins of the city.

Lot met them in the gate and invited them into his home. A hospitable man, he washed their feet, prepared a feast, unrolled fresh pallets for their sleep.

But before they lay down, the men of Sodom — "both young and old, all the people to the last man" — surrounded Lot's house.

"Hey! Aramean! Give us that sweet man-meat! Beautiful, and ripe for a screw!"

Lot went out to argue.

"Look, I got two daughters, virgins. Take the girls, and leave my guests alone."

"Bite your eyes! Get out of the way!"

The men of Sodom drove Lot backward.

But the angels snatched him inside and blinded the Sodomites outside. They became fools falling over each other.

In the morning the angels told Lot to take his family and run.

"Don't look back."

Don't look back—this was none other than the voice of God! "Don't stop in the valley. Run for the hills!"

Lot said, "There's a little village close by. Zoar. Get us there."

The Lord said, "Go!"

The four of them ran.

The Lord rained brimstone and a burning pitch on Sodom. He destroyed the houses, the walls, gates, streets, inhabitants, cattle and everything that grew green.

But Lot's wife looked back in pity.

DOES BOAZ RECALL THE TALE that defines the ground on which he walks? Cinders and salt and a little cave in Zoar? If the man is thinking at all, his thought occurs in the vacuums of the universe. Nevertheless, histories whisper in the ashen air around him.

From Zoar, Boaz ben-Salmon wanders around the southern end of the Salt Sea.

Days later find him moving like a jackal north along its western coast. Miles ahead of him there is another oasis at En Gedi. But before he can get there for food and water, the way turns treacherous. It climbs suddenly up from the sea where there is no beach, only tremendous stone cliffs rising straight out of the water.

Boaz goes a thousand feet up rough rock. Up steep cuts of dry wadis, then down a loose scree, huddling on shelves of rock at the edges of deep defiles. At night the gaunt pilgrim sleeps in one of the caves that honeycomb the limestone escarpments.

WHEN SALMON ATE PARCHED GRAIN, he tended to nibble the kernels between his front teeth, cracking them one by one. He would frown and look down his nose, crossing his eyes as if he could study the trifling bites behind his lips.

His jaw worked fast as a rabbit's. His moustaches twitched like the feelers of a locust—but solemnly. His papa chewed so solemnly, it made his little boy laugh.

To Boaz his papa *was* a locust, snicking its food with all its little mouthparts.

Bozy would giggle and put out his pointer finger to touch his papa's whisker-tips.

"What?" his father would say. He'd pull his face back from the toddler and bark, "What? What?" with such quick bewilderment that Boaz fell down laughing because he loved his papa so much.

At night the child stole from his pallet to his father's. He slipped under the warm robe in order to smell the grown man's smell. Here the child was safe from all evil, and Salmon's snoring was a love song.

A FULL FOUR HUNDRED FEET ABOVE THE SEA, on the lower slope of a predominating cliff, a spring of fresh water pools and feeds a fertile soil. Like an island growing green trees in the midst of a rocky waste, the oasis at En Gedi supports a handful of hardy families.

En Gedi: "Spring of the Young Goat."

Boaz avoids people. Nor do they speak to the bone-man when he comes and plunges his whole upper body underwater. He comes up whipping his hair into a dazzling loop of water, then lies belly-flat on the rocks around the pool, and drinks like Gideon. Then the man stands naked under the wisps of the waterfall. Name of the *Lord!*—an offense to the eyes of an Israelite! No woman, no *man*, will look at the derelict after that.

Their pleasant place, their Eden, has been violated by the serpent's corruption.

Date palms grow as tall as the pillars of Egypt. Vineyards here produce fruit fatter than the fruits of Bethlehem. Balm trees flourish. The oil pressed from their fruit makes a medicine so superior that Naomi will use no other kind, despite the expense.

Boaz dens in a cave on En Gedi's slope. He spreads fresh dates on stones where they dry under a hard sun, then he sits on his heels and hangs his arms over his knees like sticks broken on the kneecaps. His face is as vacant as salt. He waits. In time he cracks a heap of almond shells, dropping the nuts into his pack. He pounds figs into hard small loaves. He strings the dried dates on cords which he hangs around his neck.

If he were a man of sensations, he might have taken pomegranates too — for the color and the taste and the play of their slippery seeds upon his tongue. But Boaz lacks delight. Nothing is pleasant, nothing unpleasant. Food is a necessity. He eats to walk. And he walks so that thought may never catch up to him.

Miriam named her daughter "Basemath, my Balm." If Boaz were a man of thought, he'd think of his sister in this garden, of her name, of her smooth affections.

He shrugs into his worn backpack. Down, then: four hundred feet down to the mineral sea; down to its narrow shore of marl and gravel, which make a jagged path under the tough soles of his feet; away from the oasis, pilgrim, and down into the wilderness where neither winds nor the sea nor the circling raptors signify. No bushes burn. No holy chronicle makes sense of a man's experience.

But no one need pity the wanderer.

Could Wisdom utter her clarifying word, she would accuse him of the profoundest self-indulgence. Whether by conscious choice or by a sloven *unchoosing*, Boaz walks separated from Israel, isolated from Judah and Bethlehem and family and every kind of human communion.

Come, behold the prodigy made manifest in Boaz ben-Salmon: absolute individuality. This man is *this* man and nothing else. He moves in no context. He is a monument unto his own bereavement.

17

Rescue, and a Recent Death

AFTER ISRAEL SLAUGHTERED BENJAMIN; AFTER THE ESCAPE of the six hundred to the rock at Rimmon; after Israel gathered before the shrine in Bethel to contrive wives for their brother tribe, Boaz prepared to join the armies marching against Jabesh-gilead. He had no misgivings. Men need women? *Virgins* would this warrior get for them.

But as he set out through the rocky forests, sunlight struck through the trees and a white flash caught his eye. The white took shape, and Boaz recognized a donkey. His father's donkey.

He turned aside and approached the beast. Its head hung low to the ground. Grazing? No, not grazing. Nuzzling a man who lay motionless on the ground, the donkey's reins coiled around his neck.

Boaz froze. It was his father. An arrow projected from Salmon's skull, its bronze point two inches into the bone. Very little blood. The old warrior's eyes were open.

"Papa!"

Salmon's eyes twitched, seeking the sound.

Boaz dropped to his knees and clasped his hands as if in awe-ful reverence. Suddenly he leaned forward and placed his hands over Salmon's cheeks.

"Oh, Papa."

"Boaz? That you?"

"Can't you see?" Boaz snatched his hands back. "You can't see me!"

"Hush, boy. We should sleep now."

"No! Why?"

"Nighttime, Bozy. I've eaten enough."

"You're wounded. Papa, stay awake. Stay with me."

Salmon closed his eyes. The tip of his tongue ran moisture over cracked lips.

"Wait! Talk to me!"

An infinite smile formed in the thicket of his father's beard. Of its own accord, the man's right hand rose up and touched his son's cheek. Boaz felt the brush of dry flesh. His father reached higher and tapped his fingernails on the rim of the helmet his son was wearing. Boaz jerked to the side.

Salmon's hand was left in empty air. Slowly it sank again.

Boaz tore off the helmet. He grabbed the neck of his mail shirt and ripped the linen down the middle, scales flying like sparrows.

Salmon released a long exhalation.

Boaz seized the shaft of the arrow lodged in his father's skull and yanked it out.

The man jumped and began to thrash. His eyes sliced open. He bared his teeth, growling, snarling.

Boaz picked up the helmet, thinking to press it as a protection on his father's head, but blood welled up in the arrow-hole. Blood ran into Salmon's ferocious hair. The violent convulsions whipped blood across Boaz's face and chest. Salmon gnashed his teeth. Blood filled his eye sockets. He blinked and blinked, but couldn't wash the red away.

Boaz clapped his hands on either side of his father's skull to hold it still. He tried to run a thumb over the cherry-red eyeball, but the bright blood kept pulsing through his fingers. With a cry he squeezed hard to keep the lifeblood in.

Salmon's head was locked immobile. His body shuddered from the neck down and the convulsions left him. All at once he was calm and the forest was quiet and leaves were rustling in a light wind.

Though his head was fixed as if between the paws of a lion, Salmon opened his eyes and found his son's eyes.

"Thank you, Bozy."

But a spasm seized the younger man's stomach. A thread of bile rose into his mouth. Boaz wadded the mail shirt into a pillow he put under his father's head. Then he picked up a stone and began to beat the helmet, cracking the rawhide.

Only the sound of his father's voice stopped him.

"Keep my name," Salmon murmured. "You will pass it on to your firstborn son." His limbs relaxed. His face, wine-dark, was sinking into repose. "You are my life now."

Boaz's swallowed bile and guilt and grief.

"Let me," his father sighed, "kiss you...." but passed into sleep before he could.

The donkey nodded its head. Boaz saw that the reins still wound around Salmon's neck. He ought to unbind the cords. But his hands were bandages against his father's death.

A CHILD SAT BALANCED IN a fig tree, finding the holes on a flute. The fig tree was his hiding place. Whenever the elders assembled in his house, he climbed high enough to hear them in the upper rooms. Or when the Women of Bethlehem cooked meals in the courtyard, he crouched stone-still among the shiny leaves of the lower branches.

Sometimes the parents of young, unmarried women came calling. The severity with which his father drove the boy away from these conversations troubled him. It was a lighthearted game to eavesdrop on men who drank beer in the upper room. He liked the feelings of superiority when nobody knew that a boy was watching. But the conversations his father had with young women—they scared him.

On this particular day, however, no one came to visit. His father was in the house alone. He blew flute notes.

Bozy loved the old fig. It had lived long and grown twenty feet high. Of course, it cluttered the courtyard with twigs, dead leaves, sheered strips of bark, dirt-rot. The boy and his papa cleaned the flagstones together. Father had threatened to chop it down. But Boaz knew it was a false threat. Because the fig had been planted by their ancestor Amminadab, a man who had walked with Moses and fought with Joshua, and who was himself a descendant of the patriarch Judah.

Suddenly the sky grew black, and a chill wind fresh-
ened, and behind that came the slap of a hard wind, and
Boaz dropped his flute and grabbed the branch beneath
him and locked his legs around it.

Soon the black cloud was spitting lightning, and the
wind roared with steady violence.

"Papa!"

Thunder followed the lightning. Rain followed the
thunder, stinging like bees.

"Papa! I can't—"

The tree bowed down, then swooped up. The boy
gasped, terrified. Rain was a thousand needles, stabbing
his eyes.

"Boaz?"

"Papa!"

There, through the leaves—his father stood under the
fig tree, spreading his arms.

"Bozy! Jump!"

Jump?

"I can't!"

"Just let go—"

"I *can't!* You come get me!"

"I'll catch you! I promise!"

The stones of the courtyard were covered with a scud-
ding foam. Tree branches tore westward. Boaz swung so
high he screamed and pressed his cheek against the rough
bark, and that was all he knew of life. If he jumped, he'd
die.

"Bozy! Bozy! Trust me!"

No, no, no, no....

Then the wood cracked. His limb dropped a foot. Boaz swallowed his scream in horror.

"Son, listen to me! Let go!"

That was a tiny little man down there, couldn't catch a—

The limb shuddered and yawed and broke. Boaz plummeted into eternal space.

But his father caught him. His father caught him, and wrapped his arms around him, and turned, and carried a shivering boy back to the house.

The boy felt the scratch of his papa's whiskers and then the warmth of pee-water in his loincloth.

18

Days, Centuries and Millennia

IN THE LAND OF MOAB, ON THE southern slopes of a valley two miles south of Mount Nebo, there stands a mute congregation of ancient stones. *Menhirs*, so called in a language the pilgrim does not know—rough thrusts of rock, some of them twice as high as a full-grown man. It was people long extinct who up-ended these rugged monuments in loose circles like priests in tongueless incantation.

If Boaz were sensible of time or of the significance of things, he might have counted hundreds of the *menhirs* populating the slope's descent. He might have felt the weight of ten thousand years. The stones he wanders among (northerly, always northerly) give shape to primeval minds. They are canticles to the dead or to death or to the boundless skies.

They are those whose names no one remembers, but whose yearnings and whose urges have been bequeathed to every generation since—even as the taint of Adam still makes rebels of the children of today—and of you too, Boaz.

You walk through the gardens of Abel and Cain, oblivious as a lizard.

But you live after the patriarchs and matriarchs, after the Lord God uttered his Holy Name to Moses. You were born to Salmon and Nahshon. Look ahead. Do you see that mount? Raise your eyes. It is there, on the peak of Nebo, that Moses of Israel stood to see the land he would never enter.

SOMEWHAT MORE THAN A MONTH AGO Boaz wandered out of the Judean wilderness and struggled north from the Great Salt Sea into the Jordan Valley. He continued to make his way along the western bank of the Jordan River. "Struggled" because that way is covered in a dense, tangled vegetation which widens as much as a mile. People call it the *Zor*, the "Thicket." Plain folk keep to proven paths when their business takes them through it and over Jordan. The Zor is a tropical jungle: tamarisks, oleanders, willow trees; vines winding their trunks; and under the branches an impassable undergrowth of bushes and thistles, of clawing brambles and tough palisades of reeds.

Who could wander here and *not* have to struggle? Who would *want* to wander here? But Boaz is reptilian. He groped his way through a buzzing suffocating heat toward Jordan with a sickle and a myrtle-wood stick.

He shared the uneven roots with rabbits, rats, otters. Jackals fed on the small mammals. Wolves, satisfied by groundlings, left the man alone. The occasional bear grunted and shambled away.

But once in daylight Boaz stopped whacking and listened. He had smelled a putrid odor, as if caught in a faint cloud of flesh-decay. Then, at the sound of a single *tick*, he whirled, saw a leopard on a low limb, and dropped to one knee. The leopard gathered its hind paws for a leap. Boaz jammed the butt of his stick in stone and ducked. The leopard poured out of the tree. It impaled itself on the stick, but the weight of the beast drove the man flat, and its claws raked his shoulder. Immediately Boaz twisted and rolled. The talons pulled free. Up again with his sickle, Boaz sliced through the leopard's throat. Two fountains of blood broke forth. He grabbed the cat's ears and held it face-away till the body went limp.

Boaz sat down. He looked at the predator. He looked at his own coat of blood. And for the moment a certain puzzlement entered his eyes.

The leopard was maybe a hundred pounds. Why would it attack a man in daylight? Could it have sensed disease? Abject weakness in an unusual prey?

Boaz glanced down with a flicker of awareness.

Some of the blood was his own, running from the punctures in his shoulder and mingling with the cat's. Between the joints of his thumb and his forefinger Boaz squeezed out as much fresh blood as he could. There was a small patch of wild garlic behind him. He crushed the cloves and rubbed the wet mass hard into his wounds. By the time he'd finished nursing the wounds, the pilgrim's capacity to know had guttered and gone out.

Finally Boaz came to a ford east of Jericho and crossed

the river. Eastward, thereafter, to the cemetery of the *menhirs* and the foot of Mount Nebo.

Look up. Just as you looked up to the leopard and were startled into sense. Boaz! Look up to the summit of Nebo. Can you recall the song Naomi sang? — of the arrival of Israel on these eastern shores of the Jordan? over which they entered the promised land? after forty years a-wandering in the wilderness?

Son of Salmon, you need no longer *imagine* the tales of the tribes. You stand upon the land itself. Their people crowd around you. Listen to the grind of the sandals of a single man. Count his slow steps. He is very old: Moses, walking the path on which you walk, but *up* the mountain. This is his funeral march.

THE PATH THAT WINDS BACK WESTWARD from Nebo has been traveled so many centuries by beasts heavily burdened, that it lies as a bare depression in the earth. Perhaps for this reason alone Boaz shuffles along its channel to the Plains of Moab.

From noon through the hours until the sunset glares in his eyes, Boaz wanders. The land levels out. In twilight he comes upon a broad, unforested plain and could, if he knew it, scan a space more generous than he has seen since the Negev; but that was dry. This is grass.

Twenty paces off the path he lies down. His pack becomes his pillow, and the pitiful shreds of sackcloth his blanket. The stars above envelope him. But he knows nothing of the immensity or the cosmic covenants of the Creator.

Boaz neither sleeps nor thinks. He lies inert.

Get *up*, man! At least acknowledge the daybreak sky. You think you're solitary in all this rolling landscape? As unaccompanied as the broom tree in the wilderness?

Boaz! Break your bitter fast. Pay attention. The Plains of Moab murmur and laugh and shout in cheerful voices. A hundred thousand tents of the young of Israel, fresh from liberation and forty years in the wilderness! You are *not* a reed in a windless land, from whom a single, slender shadow stretches west on a barren plain and clocks the slow rotation of the sun.

Who are these, pilgrim? Who are these clothed in happy anticipations? And whence have they come?

Young men and young women sit on the ground facing a central eminence upon which an old man stands. Moses raises his arms and speaks, and in a sacred manner his voice carries to every one among the tens of tens of thousands.

"Hear O Israel," *the old man intones.*

This is the will of the Lord.

"Hear O Israel! The Lord our God, the Lord is one, and you shall love the Lord your God with all your heart, and with all your soul, and with all your might."

Multitudes murmur assent.

"And these are the words which I command you this day. Keep them upon your heart. Teach them to your children. Talk about them when you sit in your houses and when you walk by the way and when you lie down and when you get up. Bind

them as a sign upon your hand. Set them as frontlets between your eyes. Write them on the doorposts of your house.

"God has promised you a land. Now he is giving you that land.

"Behold! I have set before you life and death, blessing and curse. Therefore, choose life, that you and your descendants may live, loving the Lord your God, obeying his voice, and cleaving to him."

After that grand admonition, the Lord God speaks to Moses alone, saying: Climb Nebo. Lean on your staff. When you stand on the crown of the mountain, turn. Look west. View the land which my people have longed for ever since the stars of Abraham.

So the Lord showed Moses a kingdom: Gilead as far as Dan; Naphtali; the regions of Ephraim and Manasseh; Judah, its wilderness and hills, the Shephelah and all the land as far as the Western Sea; the Negev and the Valley of Jericho, which is called the city of palms, even as far south as the Oasis at Zoar.

Moses, the servant of the Lord, died on Nebo. God himself buried his prophet in the valley. To this day no one has known the place of his grave.

19

The Angers of Young Boaz

MIRIAM WAS IN LABOR, MOANING IN THE ROOM that he, Boaz, and his father had shared for sixteen years. Salmon's young son could hear the midwife and that flutter of females clucking and fussing around her. Miriam's mother and Miriam's aunt. No kin of *his* in there!

It was cold and raining. He lay stubbornly in the stable outside, while up in the room on the roof his father sat and stood and paced and sat again. A strong man made weak by anxiety, a courageous man reduced to whimpering. As long as Boaz lived, his father had never, *never* shown weakness. Now look at him. He'd been beaten stupid.

A LITTLE MORE THAN A year ago, Salmon came home with strings and pegs and a broad smile. He began to dig three trenches in the compound. Against a wall of the main house they made a square. Then he and Boaz carried field stones back to the compound. They set these into the trenches. Salmon was laying a new foundation.

It was to be another room. But his father wouldn't say what the room was for.

Boaz asked.

Salmon answered, "For the love of my son," and kept on building.

He molded and dried his own clay bricks with his own fresh straw, then built them row upon row, truing the corners with a plumb line.

For the love of my son.

Boaz tingled with sweet anticipations. A gift, surely. A very important gift, by the size of it. All through the month before the Passover, Salmon harvested the fields faster than ever in order to make it home an hour before the dark.

Young Boaz would pause and lean on his hoe handle and consider the possibilities. He had just turned sixteen. That's one clue. Here's another: ever since the latter rains Papa had been leaving the house long after dark—but for no reason Boaz could figure. Elders meet in the daylight. Hosts and guests sit down to their feasts before twilight. These days his father should have required *more* sleep, not less; should have shown signs of the physical stress. Yet his health was solid, his face ruddy, his briar-like hair concealed beneath a turban freshly washed. He was skipping sleep for ... what?

All at once Boaz burst into laughter. He dropped the hoe and did a stomp-dance among the weeds. He *knew* what that was.

Marriage!

Salmon had found the maiden for his son. Salmon was

off negotiating a dowry and a bride price with the parents of the boy's bride-to-be—even while he constructed the room in which to place a wedding bed. Negotiations were always slow, requiring many visits to talk about anything else, except the true purpose of the visits.

But the time was coming, and Boaz walked on winged feet and clapped his father on his back—and his father returned the clap with a true embrace, and Boaz loved the smell of the strong man's sweat. Oh, how happy Salmon was for his only son, Boaz.

Salmon went out and killed a gazelle, skinned it, dressed it and brought it home.

The next morning two of the Women of Bethlehem arrived in Salmon's courtyard and began to prepare a savory meal of the gazelle meat with vegetables and honey cakes, while young Boaz, in mute delight, bathed himself and trimmed his few soft whiskers and anointed his hair and stood in the upper room very still in order to shine when the woman came. Well, and to watch the lane below.

The two women from Bethlehem had already begun to carry up bowls and dishes for the feast this afternoon.

Then here came Salmon his father, striding triumphantly.

Who was the elder woman beside him? Why, the widow Rizpah. She had a story of her own to tell—tremendous courage while her sons lay murdered on a hillside. She spread sackcloth on a rock, and from the start of the harvest to the fall of the rains she fought off the carrion birds and beasts of the fields for the sake of the corpses of her unburied children.

But Boaz was past remembering, past watching Rizpah

too. Behind his father and the woman leaning on his arm floated the slender figure of a maiden, her face hooded and in shadow.

They entered the courtyard, and he lost sight of them.

He heard human purrings below. The food behind him was steaming and ready.

Then Salmon called out, "Boaz! Come down and speak to Rizpah, daughter of Aiah — and meet," he said in a rather husky voice, "meet her daughter Miriam."

Boaz did not bound down the steps (as his heart urged him to do), but descended with the whistling carelessness he imagined older, more experienced men would use. He entered the courtyard and bowed to Rizpah. His face was flushed with fear and joy, but he did not cast his eyes on the young woman standing behind her mother.

Salmon said, "Perhaps—" he cleared his throat. "Perhaps, son, you've noticed I've been visiting the widow Rizpah."

Boaz was a house post. He could not move.

"Perhaps you know the reason for my visits."

He kept his face fixed forward. He would not, he would not, he would not actually *look* at the maiden.

His father said, "Marriage."

Gangly Boaz almost swooned. He knew it. But he hadn't *heard* it before. Marriage.

"Boaz? Son? Haven't you anything to say? Are you disappointed?"

And the cord snapped: "Oh, Papa, no! I'm happy! I'm dancing with thanksgivings!"

Now he permitted himself a glance at Miriam. Lord,

what a match! Good strong hands, good large feet, hips bold enough to bear thirteen sons and daughters, an oak fifteen years old. It wasn't that he loved her. There'd be time for that. But here was one with whom he could work Salmon's flocks and fields till the man grew old and he, Boaz, with such a woman as this, could take over with a blooming assurance.

He puffed out his chest. Boaz ben-Salmon—today he has become a man.

Salmon said, "You amaze me." He stepped forward and put both hands on Boaz's shoulders. Man to man, they were the same height. "Any other son," he said, his eyes glistening, "might have been angry, might have fought his father for choosing to marry another wife in place of his first." Salmon kissed him. Boaz felt the whiskers. "Oh, Boze, you are an obedient, modest young man, and I love you."

Salmon turned from Boaz and moved to Miriam and slipped his hands inside her hood, around the nape of her neck.

She dropped her eyes. The woman had blunt eyelashes.

Salmon said, "I have Rizpah's permission and her blessing. She will be housed and fed for the rest of her life. Miriam and I," he said with obvious affection, "will marry on Wednesday after the Passover."

On midmorning of the wedding day, Salmon and his groomsmen processed from his house with garlands and boisterous song to meet Miriam's cart and her bridesmaids.

It was a fine blue day. All the citizens of Bethlehem had laid their work aside to give themselves over to jubilation.

Timbrels and finger-drums, palm branches and rose petals, the bride and her bridegroom met before the gate in
Bethlehem's village square. A goat was turning on a spit.
Young girls whirled. Young men made signs and winked at
them. Children ran like lambs on the hillsides, and Naomi
strummed her harp. Salmon had asked Boaz to play on his
pipe, but if the young man obeyed, his music was drowned
in the general festivities.

A feast had been prepared at Salmon's house. Music
and riddles and stories, eating and drinking long after the
wedded couple retired to their freshly plastered, brightly
painted, cinnamon-scented bedroom.

"To Salmon's!"

"Dance and laugh and run and tumble to Salmon's
place—"

"—before we die of thirst!"

But people stopped and fell silent outside of Salmon's
house.

Someone had chopped down the fig tree in his courtyard. It had crashed through the stable roof and snapped
the donkey's back. By old habit the beast was dragging
its hind hoofs through sticks and leaf-rubble, rolling its
eyes, throwing its head in an effort to heave its body up to
standing. Dutiful. Uncomplaining.

The walls of the new room had been beaten through
with a sledgehammer. The bed had been turned upside
down.

Salmon gazed at the destruction. Then with a sort
of wonder he saw that the tables and all the food were
untouched. The feast was ready, but the guests went home.

Rizpah and Miriam withdrew. Salmon was left to suffer the scene alone.

A week passed. A month. When Boaz returned he neither spoke to his father nor looked at him. Wordlessly, Salmon handed his son tools appropriate for the season. They went to work.

Salmon began to rebuild the side room that had been destroyed.

He broke the silence. "Boaz," he said, "this time the room is for you."

Boaz said, "I *had* a room. I had a whole *house!*"

The young man stripped poles for another stable. He threw the thing haphazardly together, and chose thereafter to sleep where the goats fed.

AND SO IT WAS THAT Boaz woke in the middle of a cold wintry night, hearing whimperings he thought were signs of a sick ewe lamb. He shifted position and immediately realized that the sound was coming from the old room opposite the stable. It was Miriam: scarcely nine months after the wedding, fat with the old man's issue; breasts lolling, swollen, unlovely; chins and cheeks overblown; feet like flagstones.

So this was the night when the witch would have her way—and her whelp.

A long ungodly moan crossed like cats from the house to his stable. Boaz sat up, restless with resentments.

He heard a scuffling in the courtyard. The dark door

opened, framing the figure of that hard-nosed Naomi as she entered, and the door thumped closed again.

Men were murmuring in the upper room, sitting vigil with his father: Elimelech, Mahlon, Chilion, Roth, Armoni, one or two whose voices he couldn't decipher.

Large drops of rain began to plump the courtyard stones.

Suddenly a scream brightened the night.

Boaz didn't need to imagine his father's reaction. He *saw* the man descending with a tallow candle and crossing the courtyard.

"Bozy," the man said. "Come up and sit with me."

Boaz lay down and didn't answer.

Salmon knelt. He spoke in a womanish, wheedling manner.

"I know she's not your mother. But she's my wife, and I'm your father, and she's in danger. Sit with me."

Boaz glanced at the candle.

"Watch out," he said, "or you'll set everything you own on fire."

Another scream unfurled from the birthing room. Salmon gasped. In candlelight Boaz saw true fright in his father's face—and that caused *him* to wince.

I don't want it. I don't want it. I don't want it.

And here came another woman dashing through the rain, opening that mystic door and closing it behind her. Milcah. Naomi's minion.

He raised up on an elbow. His father was gone, leaving an odd emptiness behind.

Boaz got up, and cracked his head against a low beam,

and dropped to his knees. "God! God!" He rubbed the pain with the heel of his hand—and then was astonished to feel the choke of tears in his throat.

He crawled on all fours into the rain and stood up, grateful for the wind and the winter in the courtyard. The cold stingings steadied him.

What? What, he wondered, was that low moaning sound? Why, the men, chanting *Hosanna, hosanna.* "Lord save us" like children and idiots hiding from the demon Resheph. In God's name, how could a covey of women busy in secret change warriors into sucking, mewling kittens?

And Miriam herself, young as a plump apricot—how could she snatch his real father away? Salmon, shot down in his thirty-seventh year.

A fresh red shriek knifed through the courtyard. Seconds later Rizpah emerged and walked blindly past him. She'd left the door standing open. He could see inside. Some sort of barrier was broken. So when the woman returned dragging a piece of furniture behind her, he picked it up, pulled it away, and walked straight into the room.

Miriam lay on pallets, her knees up, her head pressed back against the farther wall, her belly a mountain. Miriam's eyelids were squeezed as tight as crying, and her lips retracted in a wolvish snarl. This was the source of the screaming.

Boaz let go the wooden board. It clattered near Miriam, who showed no reaction. Was there no piercing the woman-spirit?

Naomi said something. *Holy,* she said. *Holy things.*

Boaz said, "I just want to see."

Naomi's assistant threw a cover over Miriam's belly and knees and down to her ankles. It left the laboring woman's face central in the lamplight.

Hissing. Now Miriam was hissing like scorpions. It raised the hairs on his arms.

Naomi was talking. He caught a piece of the language: *Curse you in the name of Lilith.* The fuller room swam into the young man's vision, all the women in their humid room. Spells for crushing a strong man's soul.

But not *his* soul, by God. Boaz grabbed an oxgoad from Rizpah's pitiful fingers. He fixed his eyes on the midwife to prove the dominance of his powers and his will. He refused to flinch from the fierce challenge of her looking.

And Miriam, central, surrounded by the others, only *seemed* small. Like an adder she had ruined his father, but to him her bite was a blade of grass.

Boaz swung the oxgoad at the iron-wood doorframe which such force it bent the goad, but scarcely marked the frame. Hissing, he stalked outside.

Men above the house, women inside, and he was the warrior true enough to hold them all, *all* their timorous, pewling purposes in contempt.

20

Five Virgins and a Matron

BOAZ LIES IN A DEPRESSION BETWEEN TWO rough roots of an enormous oak. He is aware. The oak looms in the middle of a forest. He's aware of these things. A silver moon watches through the lattice of high branches and casts small rags of pale light on the forest floor.

It's the fire in his shoulder that shocked his mind awake. The flesh is swollen hard as a cucumber. He must have moved his arm in his sleep. The motion sent him into transports of pain. He howled—then cut the sound. His tongue's tacky. He's profoundly thirsty. He shivers, but suffers the cursings of a fever, both at once. And he murdered his father. This enormity overwhelms every other physical affliction. It is a terrible anodyne.

The moon withdraws. Sight closes down. Boaz sinks into a damaged sleep.

The pilgrim dreams the voices of young women. They sing a trouble of dove-song in the distance, cooing and lamentation.

In the knowledge that dreams impart, the restless

sleeper knows that the singers are young and few and virgins.

Now sunlight reddens the vision behind the pilgrim's eyelids.

Someone whispers, "Get back." This voice hangs above his lying place. "Girls, stand behind that hillock, or you'll pollute yourself."

Boaz feels a warm breath wash his face. He can hear the breathing of someone concentrating over a task. He tries to turn his head away.

"Hold still." Fingers grip his temples. "Hold still." By the sound of her command, this woman is older than the virgins of his dream.

A thin line of coolness touches his shoulder. All at once it slices the skin. It's the pressure, not the cut, that opens his eyes—but then the pressure eases, the swelling deflates, and through a gummy sight he sees yellow pus mixed with a serum of blood running from the fresh wound.

Tough woman-fingers press the swelling on either side of the cut, and *now* the pain returns like wrath. The woman expresses more and more of the fluid.

Boaz realizes that he is weeping.

A moist cloth comes down and starts to wash him. He looks up: a squarish face, a woman concentrating on nothing but his wound; no time for his eyes. She tips a small, fluted jar over the trench she's cut into the shoulder. Vinegar burns. Darkness spreads from some point in his brain. The woman has grey eyebrows and wiry grey hair and a prominent nose, all of which dissolve into his dreaming.

Boaz wakes clear-headed and knows that his body has been rearranged.

His back is propped up against a mat of willow branches. His shoulder is thickly bandaged. The bandage holds a poultice against his wounds, growing hotter and hotter. Beside him someone has left water and five barley cakes.

And he's been washed. His whole *person* has been washed, as women do for a corpse or for a baby newly born.

He knows this: he is in Gilead.

Pebbles grind and clatter lightly on larger rocks. Halfway up a slope in the forest, watching him, sits the stolid figure of his nurse. He lifts an unsteady hand. She nods briefly, stands and turns and climbs. Five young maidens file behind the matron. The virgins.

Once more the pilgrim is weeping, overcome by a boil of emotions.

Five maidens, no more than thirteen years, are wandering the mountains, bewailing their virginity. They have begun to bleed the bloods of dying and of life.

Through the veil of a dreamlike darkness, Boaz has learned the story of their ritual. This is why he's crying.

Jephtha was a judge in Israel, a son of Gilead, but driven out of his country because he was the son of a prostitute. Maybe, too, Gilead feared a natural leader.

Jephtha gathered a band of men, tough, keen, loyal, organized, quite able to outfight lawless rioters or the most righteous of citizen militias.

Then the Ammonites began to oppress Gilead. They crossed the Jordan into Judah and Benjamin, and harassed Israel for eighteen long years.

Finally the elders and the chiefs called for Jephtha and salvation.

"You hated me," Jephtha answered. "Banished me from my country. Screw you. Go drink the swill of your self-righteous shame."

"Son of Gilead, please. Triumph just this once, and we'll make you the head and ruler of all the territories of Gilead."

Jephtha was persuaded. As natural a diplomat as he was a leader, he approached the king of the Ammonites and offered him a bargain.

"Here is my proposition," he said. "If you accept it, we'll make an easy peace. But if you refuse it, the consequences will be on your head, not on mine."

The king refused. Jephtha rejoiced. Oh, how he loved a lusty adventure!

And to fix the victory, he called on the God of Abraham, Isaac, to bargain with him as well.

"Give me the Ammonites, and I will give you the best burnt offering I know how. The first creature I see on my arrival home, **that** shall be yours."

Well, and it was a glorious campaign. Jephtha prevailed, overthrowing twenty cities, and destroying the Ammonites in a roaring great slaughter.

Home he rode, the trumpets of conquest in his ear.

Now the gallant new ruler of Gilead had one child only, the daughter of his heart and his every consolation.

And she loved him with the very same fervor.

Therefore—as has been the custom in Israel ever since they crossed the Red Sea and the sister of Moses danced praises

unto the Lord God, their redeemer—Jephtha's daughter came
out dancing to the slap of timbrels and singing and laughing.

When Jephtha saw the maiden he reigned back his mount.
The mighty leader dismounted as one who has been van-
quished. He took hold of his tunic and tore it from the throat
to the groin.

"My daughter, you have crushed me! You're killing me! I
made a vow to God. I swore to sacrifice the first creature to
meet me home."

The maiden's laughter died. She watched as her father sat
down on the ground, throwing dust over his head, rubbing it
on his face and naked chest.

Finally the daughter said, "You opened your mouth to the
Lord," as if affirming the thing he had confessed. He said it,
she said it, it was so. "You cannot take it back." She placed the
timbrel in her father's doorway and tightened the robe around
her body.

She said, "Let me alone for two months, that I may go wan-
dering on the mountains, and bewail my virginity."

Abject Jephtha said, "Go."

She departed, she and a number of her closest companions,
and bewailed her virginity. For the maiden, her first menses
was the end of life. For them it was the end of freedom.

After the two months had been observed his daughter
returned to him, and Jephtha did according to his vow.

Since then it has become a custom that at the beginning of
their first flow, that the daughters of Gilead go out upon the
mountains and lament the nameless daughter of Jephtha four
days in the year.

Boaz sobs and sobs until there is no water left in him.

21

A Sword in One Hand
and Hyssop in the Other

THE PILGRIM IS WALKING NORTHWARD.

On the western sides of the slopes of Gilead rainfall is abundant. The land produces rich crops of cereals, olives, grapes. Day by day Boaz regains strength. Balm trees flourish here too. He takes advantage of their ointments.

Every time he changes his bandage, Boaz relives the severity of the tale of Jephtha's daughter. He inhabits it. But he'd change the ending. *He* would be the maiden's father. With a pike and a sickle he'd make a sacrifice of his heart, his iniquitous heart in the place of his purer, lovelier, sinless heart.

It's an easy descent into the gorge of the Jabbok River. In a thin ribbon along those banks Boaz finds soil richer than any other he has tasted or crumbled in his hands. The finer the food, the faster his healing. And here there is no want for water.

Refreshed, he scales the northern wall of the gorge.

Refreshed, except in his soul. For he *is* Jephtha, but wicked of his own accord and not in obedience to some vow. A fraud in war, a killer of his own kin, a patricide.

BOAZ WALKS TWO DAYS FARTHER north along the east side of the Jordan another fifteen miles. The river wanders. His passage is slow. Boaz doesn't mind the time.

Ahead and off to the right, the pilgrim sees an uneven city wall, its western portion golden in the setting sun. He slows his pace, then hesitates, mistrustful of people—mistrustful, rather, of himself in the company of people.

He scans for the gate and finds it, its stones exploded, its posts blackened by fire. Then he smells the scorch of a horrible burning. More than its gate, the city must have gone up in flames. And is forsaken.

Isn't this what he has wanted? To avoid places of population? Yet the absence and the destruction and the scrabble of jackals inside—these trouble his spirit.

Boaz steps over the trash that was the gate. No torchlight in the streets. Houses battered and black. His tread sends rodents scurrying through the rubble. Jackals curl their tails between their legs and steal away with backward glances.

Boaz has awoken to more misery than his soul can endure.

I call heaven and earth to record this day against you, that I have set before you life and death, blessing and cursing. Therefore choose life. . . .

In a moonless darkness Boaz rounds a corner, and a small flame focuses his sight. He doesn't think. He doesn't decide. He steps on the slick entrails of some dead thing and walks toward the unsteady light.

The lamp goes out. The window darkens.

Again with no thought Boaz lifts his good arm and says, "Hello?"

From another house a voice growls, "Go away!"

Boaz turns in that direction.

As if he's being watched, the voice yells louder, "We got the weapons to kill you! Go!"

He would. He should. But he doesn't. His arm still raised as some kind of signal, he says, "I'm not here to hurt you."

"You're a thief and a robber!"

Boaz says, "But I live on mice and lizards. I don't need anything else. Water, maybe."

"Filthy! Defiled!" And now from other darkened houses: "Abominable! Unclean! The whelp of a sow!"

Curiously, the sound of human voices—the sound and the passion, no matter the meanings—produces a rough hunger in the pilgrim's guts. "Talk," he pleads with the invisible people. "I won't try to come in. I don't want anything—except to hear you talk."

Silence.

"No, don't stop. Scold me! Call me names. Spit at me. Let me hear you."

Silence takes the night and the city.

"Scream at me! Curse me!"

ONLY THE OLD AND THE very young are left in the city now. A handful of the warriors who fled a year ago, then came creeping back in shame. But there are no virgins here. There are no child-bearing women.

"The women slaughtered," says the man who took pity on the pilgrim last night, "and all our virgins stolen to be rutted by the men of Benjamin."

Boaz's host is one of the soldiers who saved his life by fleeing from the eleven tribes of Israel. He knows despair. He knows the guilt of Boaz, that it should blot him out of the Book.

In penitence for his self-serving flight, and his failure to die for Jabesh-gilead, and for the horror that met him at his return—the broken soldier could not leave the little Dannite child he once found hiding in a hyrax hole. One of her fathers had put his city to the sword. An eye for an eye was the law, justice. But there was no rage left in him. The child of his enemy must become the sign of his sorrow.

"She was four years old when I brought her home," he tells Boaz as they squat in a tiny upper room and in the morning light. The host faces him, while Boaz faces into the sun. "Such an innocent child to be heaped with, you know," the soldier continues, "you know how it is, with the furies of our maltreated people. A righteous fury—I won't argue that. I put her behind me. I took it all on me. So now: there's not a Gileadite talks to an Izzie-lover."

Last night the hapless warrior laid a moist cloth on Boaz's feet. Boaz gasped at the kindness and pulled away as if the water were boiling. But then a certain sad generosity persuaded him to give his feet back for the washing after all.

The host allows his hands to hang loose from his knee-caps. Boaz keeps his eyes fixed on his own knuckles, balled between his thighs. He cannot speak. His gratitude is so great it suffocates him. He can't so much as raise his face. Kindness, the kindness that surrounds his iniquitous self, scorches his flesh like fire.

The host says, "Hungry?"

He doesn't wait for an answer, but calls over his shoulder, "Bring the bowls, child." He puts out his arms and turns his palms up and says, "Blessed be . . ."

Light feet come tripping up steps newly sawn of cypress wood. Boaz appreciates the scent.

Quick, sweet puffings enter through the door behind the soldier. The music breaks Boaz's heart. A girl sings, "Papa."

Her father says, "Bow to my guest."

Small feet step before Boaz, blocking the sunlight. Next she must be bowing, because the sun warms the crown of his head. His eyes rise of their own accord. Now it is the top of the *child's* head he sees, so deep is her bow, her hair like a black veil hiding everything else. She's giggling. Why, it's a little joke, how long she holds the bow. She's waiting for his release.

With difficulty Boaz whispers, "Child."

Then she rises up, and light bursts from her face, and the sky explodes with such brilliance that her features are shadows on the naked sun.

Boaz leaps up, ready to fly out the window.

But three things chain him and force him still to stare into the holy light:

This is the face of his sister, Basemath!
And this face resembles the face of her mother, Miriam.
And the child is an angel of God with a sword in one hand and hyssop in the other, crying, "Come home."

Part Three

RUTH

22

The Ancient Tale

ELIMELECH AND HIS WIFE NAOMI AND THEIR SONS MAHLON *and Chilion went into the country of Moab and remained there.*

But Elimelech the husband of Naomi died.

So she was left with her two sons.

They lived in Moab about ten years, during which time each son took a Moabite wife. The name of Chilion's wife was Orpah, and the name of Mahlon's, Ruth.

Then Chilion died, and then Mahlon died, and Naomi was bereft of the men of her family, her two sons and her husband —bereft of a living and a place.

23

Leaving Medeba

THE ANCIENT MOABITE CITY OF MEDEBA was built on a singular elevation. It enjoys natural defenses around two-thirds of its wall. From the west to south to southeast, the land drops abruptly to a wide plateau. If an enemy tried to scale the severe incline, Medeba would rain down stones, fire, and angry arrows. Only to the north is there a gradual ascent whereby travelers enter the city—through a gate, under watchtowers.

Often during her sojourn in Medeba, especially after the death of Elimelech, Naomi would stand on the western wall and gaze off to her homeland. The northern portion of the Great Salt Sea lies between Moab and Judah. But because the Moabite plateau looms some three thousand feet above its waters, Naomi could see the hills of Judah and, in the night, the fires of Bethlehem.

Medeba is wealthier than any city in Judah. From her arrival the elegance has estranged her.

Its wealth derives from the caravans that stop in Medeba to rest and to trade for food and water. For the King's Highway runs right past the city. From Arabia, Sheba, Egypt in the south—from far-off India!—merchants carry exotic goods: spices, frankincense, spikenard, eaglewood; in supple leather envelopes they bring precious stones finely cut; and furniture, ebony-wood which is inlaid with silver and ivory. From Damascus they pack a fabric so firm and lustrous and unique that it is named for the city itself, "damask." From Tyre, empurpled robes for the backs of kings; from as far north as Knossos in the Mediterranean, they bring such workmanship as to take an Israelite's breath away. Naomi, however, is galled by gold molded into calves and cobras.

Something else besides the view of Judah draws the widow to the sunset side of Medeba. Caves and carved chambers riddle the topmost band of its drop-off. Mere cubits below her feet, these are the tombs of Medeba's dead.

THREE WOMEN WORK ON A NARROW LEDGE of limestone at the foot of the southwestern wall. They are replacing the bricks in the mouth of a small cavern, closing it against the jaws of wolves and the jackals. Inside on a narrow stone platform, they've laid Mahlon, the son of Naomi and the husband of Ruth. Because her mother-in-law refuses to weep, Ruth restrains her own tears. But her face betrays a grief too deep for words.

The third woman likewise is young. She *is* weeping—howling, in fact, with loud lamentations. Orpah hasn't stopped wailing since they first entered the tomb when they found the skeleton of *her* husband lying dry on that platform. She took the skull and cradled it while Naomi and Ruth cut the joints apart and placed the bones in a pit by the back wall of the cave. Chilion's bones are mixed with Elimelech's: father and son and son now occupying drought and darkness until they become dust.

Mahlon died last night. This morning the women washed his body. As a memorial for all her men—torn from her by the arbitrary hand of the Lord—Naomi spent her last penny on a thimble of myrrh. By noon the women were at the grave, bearing the dead man in.

The last brick is pounded into place. Naomi uses a staff to stand up. Without pausing to pray to the God of her ancestors, she climbs from the ledge and starts limping on a narrow path outside the wall until she reaches the city gate. She doesn't enter. Instead she sets her face to the north and descends the slow slope and travels out onto the plateau.

If her mother is aware that her daughters are following several paces behind, or that Ruth stole a goat, Naomi gives no sign of it.

They cross to the King's Highway. Heshbon is six miles north. But Naomi turns off the highway onto a rough path which cuts toward the Jordan. Ruth and Orpah are forced to moderate their steps since their mother-in-law drags a useless left leg (the hay-foot) behind the right (straw-foot). They turn toward the setting sun. Perhaps she'll go as far as Beth-jeshimoth to spend the night in safety. At nightfall the festival of the Passover of her God begins.

They make a funereal sight, these women. They wear

widows' weeds, black goat-hair robes and head-scarves folded lower than their eyebrows.

A brief rain squall wets their clothing, causing it to cloy and chafe. Yet they trudge on unheeding.

"Well, what have we here?" a male voice jeers behind them. "A brew of bubbling swamp scum!" The voice bellies forth a roar of laughter.

Ruth spins around, expecting a robber.

But it's a short-legged onion-bulb of a tradesman. He sits on a swayback. A slave with coils of shining black hair holds the goad that drives the mule. The mule is burdened further by canvas sacks slung over its haunches.

The businessman leans and thumps the skull of his slave. "What-what, Hittite?" he cries. "Two for free, I say. Two for *me*, I mean. But I,"—he kicks the mule till it comes abreast of Ruth. "I am a generous man." He reaches down and slips his fingers under Ruth's black head-scarf. "I'll give you the old fart." He whisks the scarf from Ruth's head. A wild bush of hair erupts. "Ho ho ho!" He seizes a handful. "Promise of waters below—"

Crack!

Naomi's staff nearly breaks the fat man's arm.

"She-dog!" He grabs his wrist. "I'm *playin'!* I'm just playin'."

"Playing with fire!" Naomi swings the staff above her head.

"Hittite!" the man bellows at his man. "Hit her! Snap her in half!"

But Ruth waves her black scarf in the slave's face and hisses, "A hex on you. Swell up and die."

Naomi and Her Daughters

The poor fellow is transfixed.

The tradesman yanks the goad from the slave's grip and whacks him. The slave screams. The mule breaks into a shambling run. The fat man skews sideways and struggles not to fall.

When he's well past the women, the slave having pushed his master back to balance, the merchant yells, "There's better fare in Aleppo, whores! Women *wash* in Aleppo!"

But Naomi ignores the ass on a mule. She's glaring at her daughters-in-law.

"What do you think you're doing?" She's panting for breath.

Orpah bows her head.

Ruth returns Naomi's look, not in defiance, but in imitation, with a bold sort of reverence.

"You don't think the road is dangerous?" Naomi points behind herself. "Beasts and rapists. Turn around. Go back to Medeba. You have houses in Medeba."

Orpah covers her face and starts to sob.

"Oh, my daughter," the old woman softens. "It's for the best. Lions by day and wolves and the midnight jackal. Fat fools are easy. Bandits aren't."

She limps to Orpah, leans on her staff with one arm and with the other embraces the child. "May the Lord deal kindly with you," Naomi says, "as you have dealt with the dead and with me." She kisses Orpah. For a moment it looks as if Orpah is supporting the bones of the old woman. Naomi says, "I have no sons left in me. Even if I did, you couldn't wait till they were grown."

Naomi lifts her eyes in Ruth's direction and speaks to

them both: "Don't make it worse for me. The Lord has raised his hand against me—" Naomi isn't whining. Her words state matters of bitter fact. "—and behold, that hand is a fist!" Anger strengthens her stance. "Leave me alone! My life is bad enough without you."

Orpah returns Naomi's kiss, and walks the slow road back to Medeba.

Ruth, on the other hand, sinks to her knees and covers her head with the scarf.

"What's this?" Naomi plucks at Ruth's robe. "Get up! Don't *ever* bow to me!"

Ruth does not get up. She says, "My mother."

Naomi trembles. She summons the energy to scold. "Look at your sister. She's gone the right path. Ruth, for God's sake, relieve me of the burden. I was a *foreigner* in Moab. You'd be my foreigner in *Judah*. Go away." She turns on the fulcrum of her staff and takes a step. "Let me alone. I've got burdens enough to kill me."

Ruth says, "Entreat me no more to leave you." She chants her supplication.

At the old formality of the words, Naomi pauses.

Ruth takes that as advantage, and chants:

> *Entreat me not to leave you*
> *   or to turn back from following you;*
> *Mother, Mother,*
> *   Mother of my husband dead—*
> *Where you go, I will go,*
> *   where you lodge, I will lodge;*
> *your people shall be my people,*

and your God my God;
where you die, I will die,
and there will I be buried.

Ruth concludes with an oath Naomi did not know she knew. It is not to the Moabite god Chemosh, but in the name of the God of Israel.

"May the Lord God do so to me and more, if even death should part me from you."

The furrows deepen in Naomi's face — a field plowed in bitterness, but now betrayed by rainfall.

She does nothing to acknowledge her daughter-in-law; but, head erect, the inhabitant of a howling solitude, she resumes her crippled struggle: hay-foot, straw-foot; hay-foot, straw-foot.

24

Once upon a Time,
Nearly Two Hundred Years Ago ...

A KING ROSE UP IN MOAB WHO DEFEATED THE ISRAELITES *living west of the Jordan River. King Eglon took possession of Jericho and opened a road through that "City of Palms" southeast to Medeba, where he ruled, requiring of Israel an annual tribute.*

After eighteen years, crushed almost to death, the children fell on their faces before the Lord and cried out, "Save us! Almighty God, save us from our enemies!"

The Lord took pity on them. He poured his spirit on Ehud, a stout and confident warrior, a left-handed son of Benjamin.

Thus appointed by the Lord God, Ehud offered to carry the annual tribute to Medeba himself.

Now, King Eglon was much older than the wars of his youth. For years he had enjoyed wealth and leisure, wine and rich food, and had grown too gross to walk. He waddled. And reigned from a cluster of opulent rooms on the second story of the palace—which were for him the scope of his personal world. Only in a litter on the shoulders of his servants could he go into the pleasant garden on an adjoining roof.

In preparation for his journey Ehud selected six men and ordered them to pack grain, wool, salted meats, honey on the backs of donkeys, ready to travel. At the same time he hammered on his anvil a new dagger whetted on both edges, its point as sharp as a serpent's tooth. He concealed the weapon under the robe on his right-hand side.

Three days later Ehud and his retinue walked their caravan past the sculptured stones at Gilgal, then forded the Jordan east of Jericho. They turned south and traveled the King's Highway to Medeba. Outside the city gates they were met by a band of Moabite soldiers, who gave them safe passage into the courtyards of the king.

The six Israelites took bags of silver coins from the backs of their beasts so that the Moabites could measure the tribute and make lists.

Palace guards escorted Ehud and his retinue upstairs to the king's apartments. They ran their hands down the left sides of the supplicants—since a right-handed man draws his weapon from the left—then they opened the door and permitted them entrance through a small outer vestibule into the throne room. The Israelites knelt and laid their treasures before the stool beneath Eglon's feet.

"Your highness," Ehud murmured, face to the floor.

Eglon clapped his hands. "Well done," he said. "Prettily done."

"Silver to match your glory, sir."

"Oh, look up, look up! No slave should think me cruel."

Ehud made a quick inspection of the room: walnut paneling, the door of acacia wood, the throne itself covered in damask and ornamented with Indian rubies, a canopy of

woven gold. There hung a purple curtain on the wall behind
the throne. Below its tassels the floor had been worn by walking. The curtain gave way into the king's latrine.

As for King Eglon, rolls of flesh were piled on either armrest.

Obeisances accomplished, the Israelites returned to Gilgal.
There Ehud sent his retinue and all the donkeys home. Himself
—light and unencumbered, he ran back to the capital of Moab,
Medeba.

The watchman at the gate crossed their spears against him.

Ehud blushed and tugged on his beard and apologized. He
said he had forgotten the most important thing, and pulled
from his bosom a golden, star-shaped pendant.

"It is warm. It is like a living thing, so precious is the gold,
that I didn't notice it before."

The prize opened for Ehud an easy passage to the roof, the
vestibule and into the king's throne room.

Eglon said, "It seems to me I dismissed you already?"

"Yes, sir."

"You're back."

"I really had no choice, sir."

"Why should I weary myself with a second empty
audience?"

"Two favors, Lord King."

"I have no favors for impertinence."

"The first is that you receive this humble token of my personal love for you."

The Israelite allowed the pendant to dangle from the chain
wound around the fingers of his right hand.

"Well," the king said. "Well."

"The second favor," Ehud spoke low, filled with a humble

deference, "is like the first. Let me whisper in your ear the plans my people have for rebelling against Moab, and how they seek to murder you, my gracious, merciful lord and king."

Ehud saw the flicker of fear in Eglon's eye. Fear was good.

The king commanded the guards to shut his door.

Ehud stood. "This first," he said, and hung the golden chain around Eglon's neck. "And this second." He drew close, laying his right hand on the king's shoulder.

He whispered, "The chiefs and the captains of Israel plan to kill you just like this."

Ehud drew his dagger with his left hand and plunged it into Eglon's abdomen.

The king frowned as if trying to understand something. The assassin's blade went in so deep that the hilt followed and the fat closed over Ehud's hand.

Eglon bent forward and put his arms around Ehud's chest as if he wished to whisper and answer in the Israelite's ear. The king's guts pinched the knife so tightly inside, Ehud lost it. It took a mighty yank to get his hand out, and then the shit squirted out, and Ehud jumped back, and Eglon pitched forward onto the floor.

Immediately Ehud went to the purple curtain and found a room behind it no larger than a man sitting down. Not an exit. Not a window. But under a bronze lid, a two-story shaft for the gruntings and the wastes of Moab's magnificent king, which his slaves shoveled out twice a month.

25

Celebrating Passovers Past— but the Passover Present Denied

BETH-JESHIMOTH IS THE LAST CITY IN MOAB before a traveler fords the Jordan. Two centuries ago it was here that the Children of Israel camped before they marched into the promised land (flowing with milk and honey, so to speak) to possess it.

Here, about a furlong away from the city, Naomi spreads her robe in an abandoned sheepfold. But she can't sleep. In the morning she sends Ruth into Beth-jeshimoth for fish and bread baked from dough in which good yeast had bubbled.

Today is the Passover of the Lord. The day the Lord set Israel free from slavery in Egypt. If the ritual means nothing, what's the point of keeping it? She will not fast. She will eat leavened bread. If the ritual means something, then Naomi will in bitterness defile it. She owes nothing to Abraham's God but hatred.

In the past Naomi and Milcah baked unleavened bread together. All the duties of the Passover were obeyed by her whole family—by Israel, indeed, knitting thousands into a single family.

Elimelech would go out to his flock, and select the perfect lamb, and lead it to the threshold of their door, and with a sharp knife slit its neck open. Her sons would catch the blood in basins.

Naomi roasted the lamb's meat over slow coals. Milcah crushed bitter herbs into a thick sauce.

Near evening neighbors came over, adding seven to the household number. Then Naomi, with solemn joy, swiped a brush of hyssop through the lamb's blood and smeared it across the lintel and down both posts of their door.

The Lord had commanded: *Consecrate to me all the first-born. Whatever is the first to open the womb among the people of Israel is mine!*

But all was well. On account of the blood, neither Elimelech nor Mahlon had been required by God.

Naomi returned into the firelight. Elimelech shut the door and locked it, and the angel of death beat its black wings over the roofs and did not come in.

For this too was the word of the Lord: *But every first-born son among you—my holy nation, O my kingdom of priests—you shall redeem. All the first-born of my sons I do myself redeem!*

Until in Moab, death and death and death, O thou treacherous Deity.

26

Drought

.THE NEW HOUSE THAT EZRA THE TANNER had planned for himself never did get built.

His new field produced one good harvest. Trusting in an annual abundance thereafter, he'd gone out to purchase fine raiment, baubles, a pair of Anatolian slippers, and a donkey upon which he rode high through Bethlehem.

But the field went unplowed. When Ezra saw the other farmers sowing their fields after the early rains, he filled a bag with the seed and cast it in wide sweeps across his flat ground. The others had softened their soil before the rains. His was hard and cracked. Nor could he harrow to cover the seed. The birds loved Ezra and his ways.

Other farmers chopped and hoed. Like the birds, the weeds loved Ezra's field and flourished.

Mice invaded some of the well-kept fields. And because the latter rains lasted a little too long, smut reduced the abundance the farmers had hoped for. They would eat less the coming year in order to conserve seed for the next planting.

As for Ezra, his weeds were thick and green and useless.

And so it was that the masons quit before the tanner's walls were finished.

But the coming year failed altogether. A terrific drought fell on the land of Judah. Children and the old folk wasted away. They were vulnerable to all manner of diseases. The city elders apportioned water by the cup. Mothers' breasts dried up. Babies perished unable to cry. For several years Bethlehem tried to store away a little seed to sow on following years. But every crop grew yellow-green and wilted. Finally even the seed-grain was eaten.

During these desperate years Ezra the tanner looked out for himself. He abandoned the two-room hovel outside the city walls. He reasoned that Elimelech owed him something for leaving him helpless on the land. He wasn't a farmer! He had never *been* a farmer. But before he could be taught, Elimelech left him in the lurch without a fare-thee-well.

So Ezra moved into Elimelech's house, and here the tanner is living still, but with no more care than he had taken of the hovel in which he had raised the daughter that had left him too.

When he had to, he broke into kindling the furniture, the framing, the room on the roof.

27

Rachel's Tomb

"YOU DIDN'T SPIN THE THREAD, DID YOU?"

"She spun it herself."

"I know you, Reumah. You have *always* done for that girl."

"She's married, Maacah."

"And pregnant. And you've been by her side day and night, mothering the girl-wife and her husband both, and spinning and sewing." Maacah pokes Reumah with the point of a willow rod. "Your daughter's hands are soft as a lamb snout."

The two friends sit on a roof in Bethlehem. The village is crowded wall to wall, many houses sharing the same wall. Rather than walk the winding lanes below, then, women cross roofs to gather and talk and work. Reumah's house is on a hill with a view of the road that approaches the city gate.

While they busy themselves with willow sticks and strings of willow, the cousins are watching for Eglah's return. Reumah's daughter set out yesterday morning for

Rachel's tomb. She traveled between two sisters, carrying a spool of blood-red thread.

It's midafternoon. A low, black, blowing cloud promises one more shower before the rainy season is over. No better weather for basketry. Moisture keeps the willow strings pliable. But the cloud-cover dims the distances.

Reumah says, "The only thing I did was dig the madder root and make the dye."

Maacah sports a hatchet of a nose. "The thread is red enough?"

"Scarlet."

"Long enough?"

"Maacah."

"Well, she's got to walk it round the tombstone seven times."

"Maacah, I know. Didn't I do the same pregnant myself? With Eglah, in fact?"

"Well."

Maacah's eyes are bits of glittering mica. The Lord has closed her womb. She has borne no children of her own.

The willow sticks bundled beside them were peeled before, straightened and dried stiff. They're warp rods, ribs through which the cousins are presently twining the weft strings. They tighten the weave—each basket shaped like a scooping fan, winnowing sieves—till the spaces between are tinier than grains of wheat. The barley harvest is six weeks away. The cousins will grip the rounder ends in their hands and toss the threshed harvest up into a light wind. Powdery dirt will blow away. Chaff will be whisked past the threshing floor. And the heavier barley grain will pile near the winnowing fans.

"Seven times round the stone," Maacah persists in a sort of chant, while Reumah doesn't interrupt, "makes seventy times around her neck. And seven times seventy are powers to protect the babe in a woman's womb."

Rachel died in childbirth. The Women of Bethlehem trust the pity of the Matriarch, that she will seek to save the infants or grieve with the mothers bereft.

A drizzling rain moves in from the west. Reumah pauses and peers up the road toward Bethel. She blinks water from her lashes.

Reumah says, "She's going to get sick."

Maacah pulls the hood over her head, and keeps weaving.

Reumah squints northward. Her teeth start chattering.

Maacah looks up. "You want to go inside?"

"Miserable weather. What if bandits jumped them?"

"You're the one who urged her to go to the tomb. Trust in the Lord."

"But it's cold."

"She's not alone."

Maacah scoots close to Reumah's side. She presses their bodies together. "She isn't alone. The three of them, *they're* not alone. The pity of the Matriarch covers children who carry children in a mother's mercy."

Now, when Jacob traveled back *to his grandfather Abraham's home town, and when he went to work for his uncle*

Laban, he fell in love with Laban's younger daughter, Rachel of the lovely eyes.

He asked Laban for her hand in marriage.

Laban answered, "Work for me for seven years. At the end of seven years you shall marry Rachel."

Rachel loved Jacob too. They both suffered the seven years, but separately, so that they knew each other by sight and by voice, but not by touch.

Laban's elder daughter was named Leah—she of the dull eyes.

At the end of the seven years, Jacob said to his uncle, "It's time."

"It is time," Laban agreed, and made every arrangement for a lavish wedding feast.

But Rachel saw that the wedding robe had been sewn larger than her own frame.

And on the day of the wedding itself, Laban commanded two shepherds to conduct his younger daughter to a sheepfold and to keep her there until the morrow.

Her father was planning a treachery—to break his covenant with Jacob, to give his nephew Leah's hand instead of Rachel's.

Imprisoned in the sheepfold, Rachel hated her father. Her love for Jacob—and his for her—was soon to be tormented past all righteousness.

But when she heard the timbrel and the drums and the laughter, the song and the dancing, Rachel imagined what joy Leah must be feeling, her round face concealed behind the bride's veil, and her heart broke on behalf of her sister.

For come the night when Jacob and Leah lay down to make

love, he would hear her cow-mooing voice and know the trickery and refuse to enter Leah, but will throw her out of his bed and his tent, and no one will woo her again, and she will live the rest of her life a barren woman, an unmarried virgin.

But if he went into her, the marriage was consummated. And if Leah conceived and bore a child, she would gladden her husband's heart.

Therefore Rachel began to sing by the gate of the sheepfold. She sang a sleepy lullaby. As the sun was setting, they fell asleep.

Rachel slipped through the evening. While Laban's household was still drinking itself sloppy, she crept into the wedding chamber and hid beneath the bed.

Soon the couple came into the spiced and garlanded room. Jacob whispered to his veiled bride, "O Rachel, how long we've waited. But love conquers all."

He snuffed the lamp.

Rachel heard the rustlings of bodies disrobing, then felt their weight on the bed.

Soon she heard Jacob's yearning cries: "I can't wait." He was panting. "Rachel! Open your garden. Let me, let me in—"

This was the moment. Just as she felt the bump of the thrust of his hips, Rachel cried out. Her voice, not Leah's. And Leah must have understood immediately, for she made no sound under her husband's bolting rush to the finish line.

Rachel bleated as if in pain and in pleasure. While her betrothed made love to her sister, while he laughed in the bed above her face, Rachel fought sorrow and yipped and groaned in a convincing, false delight.

She was gone before they waked in the morning.

And Jacob was angry.

But Jacob was married.

Laban was unapologetic. "Work seven more years, and I'll give you Rachel too."

"REUMAH!" MAACAH SHOUTS. "ISN'T THAT your daughter?"

Reumah grabs the parapet with both hands and blinks against the rain. "Where?"

"The mist ... There!"

Both women stare fiercely forward.

Maacah says, "I spied two of them." She points. "You see them, Reumah?"

"The one in the back—is she on her hands and knees? Oh, she's wounded."

"I don't think so," Maacah says. "I think it's a goat."

"What? A what?"

"And ... Oh, I'm so sorry."

Reumah says, "It isn't Eglah, is it?"

"No. Strangers. Foreigners. Moabites, I think."

WHEN EGLAH RETURNS TO BETHLEHEM, the red thread wound loosely around her neck, two things surprise her: that her mother rushes out sobbing so grievously it seems as if a near relative has died. And that her mother comes alone.

It should have been all the Women of Bethlehem. For it is their custom to accompany their sisters through every critical stage of life and living, of dying and of death.

28

Basemath and Her Brother, Nine Years Ago

BY HER SIXTH YEAR, BASEMATH HAD BECOME A NIMBLE GOAT on the hilltops. The daughter of Miriam and the orphan of her father Salmon, she ran when she should have walked, laughed when she should have been modest. But these things were forgiven since she loved chores as much as a swimmer loves the sea, flying through her morning duties till she had the rest of the day to herself. Games and racing, the locks of her hair blown backward like swifts skimming the sea.

Basemath's skinny legs and the pooch of a young girl's tummy endeared her to the Women of Bethlehem, every one of whom mothered her whenever she entered their houses. "Little Balm, our little Balm." Her smile showed the gaps in her front teeth.

"Did your mother pull your teeth?"

"Nope. Just popped—*bing!*—and I lost them. *Bing!*"

Actually, *Basemath* had been responsible for the loss of

her milk teeth. It was a game she played in private. A man's game. Hunting.

At four years old the child had chased the mice that ran ahead of the wheat-field reapers. She knocked them in their heads with accurate stones. But the game grew too easy for her. So she learned how to construct snares for small birds; next, traps for hares and even for the hyrax that nested in rock piles. The hunter skinned her mammal catch and brought the meat home to her mother.

What she taught herself next defied the customs of her people. Bows belonged to men. Arrows were shot by men. Hunting in the wildwood where savage beasts prowled around was altogether too dangerous for women.

But Basemath found the bow her brother had used when he was a boy. When her neighbor dressed a roebuck, he gave her a length of sinew which—in private—she used to restring the bow.

She scraped a reed straight, feathered it at one end and knobbed the other, then, to her delight, bopped a pigeon that was perched on the fig-stump in their courtyard. It hit the flagstones, its small claws upward. She grabbed it and sacked it before her mother could see what she'd done— and dashed away, giddy with her newfound skill.

Early one dawn, when Basemath sneaked out to hunt before returning to do her chores, she noticed the black form of a man—so it seemed—leaning back against the outside wall of their courtyard.

She notched an arrow. "Do I know you?" she demanded.

But the man remained motionless.

Basemath drew the arrow back to her ear. She strove for a gruff, masculine voice: "Better tell me your name."

Like wind on sand, the man muttered, "I have no name."

The answer confused the girl. Nobody has no name.

"An enemy, then?" she challenged him. "Or a guest?"

In the iron light of the east, details began to emerge. A beggar, by the poverty of his clothes. And his legs as thin as a heron's, his face soot-covered, his eyes (oh, look!) sad.

Basemath let the arrow fall. She put the bow on the ground. She said, "Maybe you want a drink?"

He shook his head. Sadder and sadder.

"I'm going to get you some bread." She turned to the doorway before he could deny her.

But he said, as if to hurry his words before he lost the chance, "I didn't keep my promise. I have to repent."

Saddest of all sadnesses.

"Oh mister man of no name, it's okay. Everything's all right."

"To beg your forgiveness," he groaned. "And your mother's forgiveness."

"You *know* us? You know *us*?"

"I told you. I promised you I would come back after the war."

The child closed her mouth. *Promised me?*

"And I sinned against your mother."

Now it was Basemath's turn to be still.

The man hadn't moved, lay there like an animal shot dead.

They made a stone tableau.

Basemath heard her mother shuffle in the house. Soon she'd go into the courtyard and blow on the banked coals.

Basemath said, "How can someone forgive a no name? God knows names. Ask him."

"A name," the beggar breathed, "blotted out of the Book of Life."

Miriam called, "Basemath?"

The man said, "My Balm."

And Basemath gasped. "Mama, come out here. Mama! Out *here!*"

The man groaned. "Lord God, I didn't want . . ."

Basemath said, "You *are*, aren't you?"

Miriam came through the door into the lane. "Girl, what are you doing outside so early?"

The man groaned again.

Miriam looked down. "Basemath, what—? A *man!* Get inside!" And to the man: "Beg in the gate. The *city* gate. Keep your hands off—"

Basemath yelled, "Mama! It's Boaz!"

Miriam grabbed her daughter's arm. "I told you. Inside."

But the girl pulled away. "Bozy!" She threw her arms around his neck and started kissing him and weeping. "Bozy, Bozy, you came back."

Her brother didn't return the embrace. He hung his head. Tears came easily these past days. He wept.

Basemath said, "But you *did*, Boaz. You kept your promise."

29

"Let Me Wash Your Hair"

NAOMI'S HOUSE IS OCCUPIED. TEN YEARS HAVE RUINED IT. Ten years and the depredations of Ezra the tanner-that-was. Naomi is too weary to argue with the slug and too broken to restore the place even if she won it back again.

Nor does she accept bed or board or help from the Women of Bethlehem. They greet her with affection. "Here is our pleasure, sisters!" they say. "Here is our pleasant Naomi home again!"

With not so much as a nod, the old woman growls, "If you call me anything, call me 'Bitterness.' For God Almighty has beaten me bitter."

As Naomi turns from the gate, Ruth hears a muttering which no one tries to hide. "The Moabite," someone says. "Mark my words, that foreigner's cast a spell on poor old Naomi."

Out of sight Naomi nearly collapses. She was feigning strength. Now she stops, leans heavily on the staff. Her mouth looks like a howl, but it's fighting for air.

Finally she limps around the wall of the city to the southeastern quarter and down a stony gradient toward a hovel as disgusting as a vulture's nest. Wordlessly Ruth follows her mother-in-law.

Here are the unplastered, wind-gapped walls of two rooms. Vegetation inside and out. A cross-beam above. No roof; the clay floor riddled with rodent holes; the "yard" a mass of thorns and thistles. There was a low fence outside, but its stones have fallen into rubble, some trundled away to fit in someone else's fence.

Naomi glances around the rubble, then limps painfully to a granite slab close to the hovel's empty doorway. She jams the butt of her staff into a sort of socket among rock, grips the smooth wood in two hands and lowers herself until she is sitting on the slab.

She folds her arms upon her hollow bosom, and quits. Naomi chooses not to stir again.

In the days that follow, Ruth works in a mute determination. She hasn't asked permission. She doesn't explain herself. The Moabite bends at the hips, her strong legs straight, and tears weeds out by root. She rakes the crumbled earth smooth. Chaff and twigs, old charcoal, crushed lime, potsherds she spreads over the inside floor, and sprays it damp, and stomps it down.

She cuts down a limb which is a natural ladder of branches and begins to lay long staves, however crooked, over the beam and wall to wall, and upon those, wide fans of tree branches, and on those stalks and a close layer of straw, and on that clay to dry in the sun.

Bats—what the Israelites call the "little foxes"—hang upside-down in the bricked corners. No matter how wildly Ruth shakes blankets at them or throws stones, they *will* return in the morning and roost. Snakes and scorpions and lizards move and breed in the interior vegetation. In a day they crawl into the fresh dry grasses of the roof.

So Ruth wanders afar gathering sticks and cakes of manure. Nearby there are chunks of rawhide. She piles the stuff in front of the doorway. She crushes castor beans, catches the oil in a cracked basin, and pours this over the pile, and sets it on fire. *Whoosh!* Even Naomi's attention focuses on white heat. When the burn-pile has been reduced to smoking coals, Ruth rakes them into the hovel. In time the noxious critters escape, and the hovel moves one more stage to becoming a house.

Naomi eats so little food her body seems to have lost its need for excretion. They live mostly on goat's milk. Sycamore figs, animal fodder such as millet, mulberries.

On the other hand, Naomi sometimes befouls herself with diarrhea. Ruth washes her. Neither woman speaks.

Oh, mother, will you ever rise up and sing again?

SOME OF THE WOMEN OF BETHLEHEM remember the Naomi that left them ten years ago. Those who had been Naomi's age, of course, perished in the long drought. But the women who knew the Hakamah in their youth were prepared to honor her again and to give God thanks that he had brought wisdom and mystery back to Bethlehem.

But *this* Naomi is a grim old crone. She comes with curses on her back. She's changed so radically that she denies her own name. Call her *Marah*, indeed. Marah, sitting in filthy black widow's weeds, hair grey and unwashed, her face as if it had been carved craggy out of boxwood.

And they have a pretty good idea who has cursed the old healer. The Women of Bethlehem can see for themselves what a parasite the dark-skinned Moabite is, sucking the spirit from their Bethlehemite. Why, she's as muscled as a man—and by the pagan god Chemosh has cursed Naomi's legs and stomach and joy and all the thought of her heart.

THE CLAY THAT RUTH SPREAD OVER THE ROOFING (sycamore branches and reeds and bundles of dried grass) is almost as hard as it will get. Now she rolls the whole roof flat, then, granted a short leisure, builds an evening fire and heats well-water.

She kneels in front of her mother-in-law.

"Mother, even the grieving eat."

Naomi rakes her scalp with all ten fingers. When she pulls them out, the fingernails are stained with blood. She sucks them one by one.

"Please let me wash your hair. Oleander and thyme, and I'll crack the lice that jump out."

"Crack the scorpion in my soul."

Ruth spends several days plastering the hovel inside and out. She whitewashes the plaster.

One evening Naomi takes hold of her staff and climbs it hand over hand until she's found her feet. Ruth grabs her mother's ratty goat-hair robe, rushes inside the little house and spreads the garment on the ground. Wordlessly Naomi sits. Ruth lights a lamp of impoverishment: its wick woven of willow seeds, its oil squeezed from castor beans.

Naomi's head sinks to her chest; then, her hands between her knees, the old woman slips sideways and lies sleeping on the ground.

Ruth sneaks into the yard. With an old ox-goad she lifts a stone jar out of a heap of burning coals, then pours water into the jar. The water makes fierce, scouring hiss. Ruth wraps a rag around its neck and carries it inside, where she fills a basin with the warm water.

The young Moabite rounds her mouth — as did her mother in Moab when Mahlon lay sick — and begins to croon "Ooooo" on a single note. Then the consoling words:

> *In thee, O Lord, do I seek refuge, Ooooo.*
> *Let me never be put to shame —*

In perfect Hebrew, a mother's lullaby:

> *Incline thine ear to me.*
> *Be thou my rock and my fortress —*

Without waking, Naomi sighs. She is an old string plucked. Ruth is a breathy flute:

> *Thou art my rock and my fortress;*
> *for thy name's sake lead me, guide me —*

Ruth infuses oleander and the parsley syrup into the warm water, cups her hands, and drizzles the solution into Naomi's hair. It's the same temperature as the old woman's body. With the next passage of the psalm mothers throughout Israel sing their children to sleep:

Into thy hands I commit my spirit—
for thou hast redeemed me, O Lord,
   O my faithful God.

30

THE PAST: Mahlon in a Nightmare
AND THE PRESENT: "Let Me Die"

NAOMI IS DREAMING OF THE SHINING SCAR that knifes Mahlon's thigh from the hip to the knee. Her son stands in the doorway, his arm raised, his back to Medeba, his face turned into the compound. Naomi can see all things. Mahlon is naked. Now the mark of his war is dead white. Now it is iridescent, like mother-of-pearl. It makes a narrow valley because the meat was scooped before the healer could stitch her firstborn closed again.

Words come buzzing like swarms of bees: *Help me, help me.*

Her son is pleading with her. But he hasn't moved. His upraised arm hasn't moved.

Mama, what will you do without me?

Knowledge, too, swarms the dreamer like dusty bits of ruin. Her husband is ashes and a handful of teeth. Chilion's skull grins on its stone table in the tomb. Mahlon alone is left.

Suddenly there are beams in her courtyard, light so bright it hums.

Naomi sees Mahlon's eyes, that they are inflamed. They

197

are fixed on her, though Naomi herself seems to be a nothing in a nowhere.

Help me. They're chewing me, myriads consuming me.

Mahlon's scar opens like a slow incision. Small red beads appear, and then, as the wound widens, showing maggots feeding on Mahlon's meat.

But you are thirty-seven. There is no half to your age. It can't be quartered. Even the Lord God can't divide the number thirty-seven.

Mahlon's leg becomes a rotten post and crumbles. For an instant the rest of the body remains upright, its arm extended. Then the second leg becomes dust and Mahlon's trunk drops. Naomi hears the thud.

Maggots become an ivory waterfall, pouring from her son's mouth and eyes.

The million worms turn into flies, and flies darken the light.

Naomi grows horrified. The horror destroys her separation.

The mother yells, *Into thy hands!* Her knowledge of medicines, her arts of healing now shoot like bolts from her fingertips. Naomi is being poured out like water.

She is lying beside her son, hugging him until the body is dust in her arms.

Nothing the healer did for her husband had saved him. Nothing for Chilion had saved him. Guilt thickens her tongue. Mahlon loved the Lord! Devoutly he repeated the great *Shema* four times daily.

Mahlon dust and ashes: this was the *Lord's* doing! He

murders the righteous! And for what? For a cackle and a hearty slap on the knee.

Her son's last exhalation, the stirring of his dust, was the spirit gone out of him.

Tear me, Lord! O you hateful God!—tear me to pieces! Kill me, or I will be the wasp in your nostrils all the days I live.

Naomi does not weep forever and forever.

RUTH SLEEPS SOUNDLY. A breeze moves in the room. Naomi shivers. Ah, her hair is wet, her contemplations hardened into a kind of iron. She's cold and can't stop shivering.

Naomi finds herself on her hands and knees. No staff, no robe, she crawls outside. The canvas curtain in the doorway slides over her back, and she keeps on crawling.

Her senses quiver, preternaturally sharp. She smells a patch of chicory, and badgers under rocks, and the death-scent of a snake.

Twice she tumbles over a narrow skirt of stone. Each time she lies still a moment, testing her legs and arms for injury. Then she continues the slow crawl.

Finally Naomi slumps under the wild branches of a broom tree.

"It is enough now." She has found and chews the poisonous oleander root. She swallows her saliva. And then the leaves. And then the pulp.

"O Lord take my life. You have laid me lower than my ancestors."

Let me perish. Let me die.

31

Shot an Ibex in Its Chest

"COME ON, BOZY! HURRY UP!"

The third year after Boaz had come home again, the rains came and the harvest improved. Now his sister was eleven years old.

"Keep up! Climb faster!"

They were scaling the steps from terrace to terrace on the hillside Salmon had worked—terraces as old as his great-grandfather, supported with stone girdlings. Orchards and vines that Salmon had weeded and pruned and harvested. Now it was Boaz who managed the plots. He knew the soil and the stones and the systems of irrigation. He repaired the broken supports with new stone. The farmer considered day with his Balm to be a break in the labor.

Basemath was a gazelle lightly vaulting the steps ahead of him.

Her happy, untroubled spirit had granted Boaz hope in hard times. He had learned to laugh again.

She wore a sling over her shoulder, packed with old wine and a few figs "for lunch, Boze."

Yesterday she had approached him with a triangular case. The tooling, the grain of it, and the well-grooved tightness were immediately familiar. He pulled the pegs and lifted the lid. Inside lay a composite bow. His father's case, his father's bow. Boaz felt an old grief.

She whispered as if it were a conspiracy, "I didn't want anyone to know."

"You kept it," he murmured, caressing the smooth composite, "hidden."

"Boaz?" Her expression begged his generosity. "I've been using it."

It was the bow case that Boaz was carrying up the hill behind his sister. Was he betraying his father? Was he taking his father's place? Or was he giving life to the memory of his father?

They cleared the terraces, and now were mounting by crannies and outcroppings the grizzled face of a mountain. She might have slipped on the loose scree and pitched backward, but Basemath never missed her step. Nimble, in love with the balanced stamina of her body—she bounded the stones in rhythms something like a tambourine's.

By his sixth year home Boaz had become a well-respected elder in Bethlehem. When a dispute required judgment, he took his place among the grey beards in the gate. He listened to everyone, the wise *and* the foolish, and only after he had settled the matter in his mind did he speak to the assembly.

But Basemath could persuade the elder to throw off solemnity and run carefree on the mountains. Her head unscarved, raven ringlets flying behind, Basemath skipped upward sure as a she-goat. She knew the switchbacks. Clearly this pathless climb was not new to her. A crosswind would press her shift against a woman's widening hips.

Look down, O pensive elder, and watch as the earth becomes one round horizon.

Soon Boaz, together with Basemath's mother, would have to negotiate for a good man to take her hand in marriage to wed her. There were one or two possibilities. At first Boaz evaluated them with confident expectations. But Miriam had reservations. At one point Miriam had dropped her face into the crook of her elbow and shook in distress.

"Why—?" But Boaz didn't finish the question. He knew why.

"Here we are," Basemath cried out in the whipping wind—on top of a small mountain bubbling with glee, twirling with her arms wide. "See?"

"Girl, you amaze me."

Basemath pointed to a number of summits higher than theirs, then aimed her finger toward one in particular. The peaks all shared the same base. None was very far from each other.

"There," she said. "Keep your eyes on that ledge. See it?"

"Yes."

"Let's eat." Basemath sat and laid out figs and parched wheat and wine. She said, "Give me the bow."

"No," said Boaz. "Why?"

"I let you carry it just because it's bulky."

"So?"

"Every other time I came here I carried it myself."

"You—?"

Basemath glanced across the mountain slopes, and jumped up. "No time to argue." She took the bow-case, twitched it open, bent the bow to string it, drew back an arrow, aimed, and shot an ibex in its chest.

What Israel called a "mountain goat": it lost its footing and tumbled twenty cubits down, pebbles clattering with it.

Basemath rummaged in her bag. She pulled out a skinning knife and handed it to her brother.

"Tell mama it's you shot the meat. Tell anyone who asks, it's you."

32

"To Glean, If You'll Give Me Permission"

AT THE TOUCH OF AN ANGEL ANCIENT NAOMI COMES AWAKE.

The angel says, "Rise up and eat."

Naomi looks and sees a little barley cake and a small cup of milk.

She eats the bread and drinks the milk. Goat's milk. She thinks the milk is sour. Then she realizes that it's mixing with the taste of her own vomit.

She lies down again and slumps into sleep.

The angel touches her a second time. "Hakamah, rise up and eat," she says, "or the journey will be too much for you."

Naomi sits up. It's daylight. She's in a small copse of rocks.

And here's another barley cake. She takes a small bite. Surprise: her mouth starts to water. The barley meal has been mixed with black cumin. It gives her pleasure.

She drinks the goat's milk.

The face of the angel swims into focus. It's Ruth, her daughter-in-law.

Ruth is saying, "If you die it will break my heart, and I will die of a broken heart. Let me hold you. Let me warm you. Let me feed you better than I've fed you before. Give me permission to go out in the fields tomorrow morning. Let me glean behind the reapers."

So after ten years Naomi returned, and Ruth the Moabite her daughter-in-law with her, from the country of Moab.

And they came to Bethlehem at the beginning of the barley harvest.

Ruth pauses on a small promontory southwest of Bethlehem. As if they are carpets unrolled side by side before her, the barley fields are ripe for the harvest.

Before sunup the reapers take their places along the back borders of the long strips of fields, borders at the foot of her promontory. The reapers are men with curved sickles. All the laborers are chatting in the coolness.

All at once, at a signal Ruth neither hears nor sees, the men go to work. They grab handfuls of stalks, cut them off below the holding hand, then lay the stalks and seed-heads on the ground behind them.

Ruth descends to the widest barley field with the greatest number of servants.

A line of women follows the reapers. They bow to bundle the stalks and to tie each bundle with pliable straws. Ruth chooses this field because the man who owns it must be wealthier than all the rest: money enough to pay for twice the workforce.

After the reapers, the bundlers. After the bundlers come young men who bind the bundles into broad sheaves which they set on end. Finally the fourth division of laborers sends up clouds of dust as they dump the sheaves into carts and wagons, then lead their oxen to the threshing floors of Bethlehem.

And so it goes as the sun rises higher.

Great jars of water have been placed at intervals from one end of the field to the other.

Ruth comes near the happy activity, cannot join the song and does not begin to glean behind the gleaners who follow the last of all.

Flint sickles swish through the stalks, feet thump rhythms, a hearty voice chants verses while a hundred peasants answer with a loud refrain:

> *When the Lord restores the fortunes of Judah,*
> **the fortunes of Judah!**
> *we are like those in a dream.*
> *Our mouths are filled with laughter*
> *and our tongues with shouts of joy!*
> *Then it is said among the nations,*
> **among the nations!**
> *"The Lord has done great things for them."*
> *Those who sowed in tears*
> **reap with shouts of joy!**

One man distinguishes himself from all the others. He

doesn't sing. He carries a boxwood club and walks at his own pace among the hired hands. They wear loincloths. They tuck their skirts up above their thighs. This man wears a breezy tunic, belted at the waist: the landowner's steward, overseeing the field work in his master's absence.

"Here!" he shouts at a young man who's popping his chest muscles in view of a covey of maidens. "Here, fool! Look over *here!* You're more ox than your ox!"

The ox that pulls the cart is grazing on good grain.

"Get to work, you bull-fart, or you'll *have* no work!"

Laborers look around, then point and whoop at the boy, who shrinks in shame.

The foreman sits down in a shady booth. Ruth walks over. She stands on the path, saying nothing, waiting to be noticed.

"A Moabite," he sneers. "What d'ya think you're doing here?"

"To glean, if you'll give me permission."

He puts forth the handle end of his club and slips it up the sleeve of her robe.

"Widow's weeds," he says. "Widows and orphans, widows and orphans, and now I gotta deal with a pagan that spits little pagans. God, I'm cursed."

Ruth withdraws the sleeve. "I am the widow of Mahlon, the son of Elimelech. Elimelech—" She speaks like an accountant offering figures. "—an Ephrathite."

"An Ephrathite," the steward murmurs. "Hmm." Naomi told her daughter-in-law that the landholder was also an Ephrathite.

Picking her way to the southeast corner of the field, Ruth passes by a fire-faced youth, busily piling his oxcart so full it'll tumble down at the first bump.

RUTH WORKS WITHOUT PAUSE, GLEANING, gathering into the bosom of her robe the heads and the straw left behind. At midday, the sun's savage heat drives her to her knees. Still she works, until she crouches down and covers the base of her skull, pulsing with pain.

She hears men's voices, one of them well-spoken and calm enough to cross the distance without shouting.

She sees that they are two, one bandy-legged, the foreman, the other tall and straight as a cedar tree.

Ruth sinks into her swimming misery. Her tongue clings to the roof of her mouth.

The tall man points at her. "Who's that?"

The steward shakes his head and spits. His answer is an inarticulate grumble.

The tall man leaves the inferior fellow behind and strides across the field in Ruth's direction.

The man wears a pure white turban wound with an uncommon elegance, its tail end free to hang down his back. His hair peeps out beneath the turban in well-cut curls. His beard is trimmed to the contours of his jaw. And his expression is straightforward. Ruth is unprepared and unable and mortified.

His shadow covers her. He waits in silence. Finally he squats beside her and says, "My daughter."

Daughter?

"Don't be afraid. I think you're sunstruck." He sets the back of his hand to her forehead.

"Don't move," he says. "I'll be right back."

What Israelite calls a Moabite "daughter"?

Across the field he unwraps his turban, dips one end into a large water jar, then loops the long cloth around his neck. He takes a flask from the booth of the foreman and a piece of fruit, then carries these back to Ruth.

As he passes, men sweep off their caps. Women bow. To everyone he says, "The Lord be with you," and the laborers answer, "The Lord bless you."

Again, he kneels, this time to help Ruth into a sitting position. He dribbles some sour wine into her mouth. It runs down her throat. She reaches for the flask, but he says, "Not so fast, Ruth." He pulls the wine away, then lays the cool cloth across the back of her neck and over her head. His turban. She wipes her face in it.

He called me by name. He knows my name.

She tries to hand the cloth back. "No, don't stop," the tall man says. "Take your time. I think I hear your cheeks crackling, dry as crackers baked on a stove." A velvet baritone. He says, "I have a small muskmelon here."

Ruth whispers, "Bless you, sir."

The man says, "See? I've conjured words from an olive tree!" Then with true tenderness he says, "You have cared for Naomi, whose husband was the best friend of my father. A Moabite and a sojourner, you care for the widow Naomi who is hateful and sad and hard to live with." He winds the dry end of the cloth around her hand. She begins to dab her ears and the nape of her neck dry.

The landowner says with soft admiration, "It is a godly thing that you do."

33

Chicory Root

"I come to get my rightful due."

Ezra, the tanner-that-was, leans doubled down on two crutches, occupying the sun-drenched space in front of the doorway. Naomi sits inside, in shadow.

Ezra has aged poorly. He is a bent old man, his bald head blotchy, the hair on the sides of his skull greasy strands whose tips prickle his neck, his yellow toenails curling under the toes. The crutches are tree branches cut to fork beneath his armpits with pegs as handholds. He wears a cord of tanned rat skins around his neck.

"Justice," he declares. "Ain't lookin' for handouts, missus. Never did do. It's payment, fair and square."

Naomi watches Ezra's person as if through tunnels polished, ancient, and extended. Diminished by the long-sighted distance, he seems a figure more curious than threatening—sticks and sinews hastily joined. He's speaking nonsense. She smiles bleakly.

Ezra takes a moment, then retracts his lips in a grin. Stumps for teeth in beds ruined by infection. He shifts his position. The grin disappears. In order to face the doorway directly he must turn his whole torso at once, humping his crutches three, four times around. The motion costs him visible pain.

"I'm a plain man, so I'll say it plain," he says. "Never was a time I didn't respect Elimelech. Now, you are a widow-woman. And you know what's what. A man like me, circumcised, he don't need treat with no widow-woman." Another grin comes and goes. "But I'm willin', see. So, then. So, on account of Elimelech, and on account of I am an honorful man, I'm gonna do you generous, missus. No need for a go-between. We'll penny-prize it right here, you and me, and come to terms, no elders and no judgments in the gate."

He stops, evidently granting her time to respond.

But Naomi dwells in another realm, observing with mild interest the faraway scene and its crooked little man.

Ezra waits. He blinks. Finally he says, "Here, now." He unties his necklace of rat skins, then spreads the string from hand to hand between his crutches. "Here, now," he says. "Gifts. Yours for the takin' and proofs that Ezra is a righteous man." The old man's flesh is pale as a fish. He works his mouth around toothless gums. Bony lumps have locked his knees and elbows at cruel angles.

Naomi sits with nothing to say.

Ezra shakes the string. He drops one end and allows the pelts to slip off within her reach. But Naomi makes no move nor acknowledges the rats' skins on the threshold.

Ezra growls: "Milcah and me. My poor daughter and me." His breathing is labored. "We helped you and yours.

She a maid to you, missus. She a *slave* on account of no payment, never! Not in my scrip, so's to notice it!" The forward thrust of Ezra's neck and the droop of his shoulders give him the appearance of a vulture, weak-footed, walking the ground.

"Mind me, woman! Mind me! I want what's owed me! You and that black Moabite stole my house! This is *my* house! I want it back!"

Naomi takes hold of the staff beside her, then, hand over hand, pulls herself up. She wobbles a moment, finding her feet. When she is steady, she moves through the doorway and over the rat skins toward Ezra—whose eyes blink rapidly. But Naomi limps past him and away from the hovel.

"Si' *down!*" Ezra screams. "Come back here!" he screams.

But, hay-foot, straw-foot, she continues moving.

Rise up and eat, or the journey will be too much for you.

"I want my house back!"

The hay-foot crunches, the straw-foot drags.

Behind her Naomi hears an awful roar and the popping of branches and something like kindling hitting the ground.

Last night she smelled a patch of wild chicory. Now she kneels and patiently loosens the soil around the bush. All in good time, she pulls the stem out with the roots.

Naomi finds Ezra lying against the whitewashed wall of the house. He's shivering and grinding his cheekbone in the dust. Under his mouth the dirt is soaked: spit-drool and snot—and tears. As best he can in his condition, the tanner-that-was is crying.

Naomi puffs on a pile of coals. Sparks twinkle. She lays manure cakes on the coals and blows again. She pours a little water into a pot, and hangs the pot from a tripod over the fire. Slowly. All in good time.

While the water simmers, the old woman bites and strips the rough skin from the chicory roots. She chops the root into fine, white pieces, then stirs them into the boiling water. Dried and crushed chicory makes a tolerable tea. But the fresh root lends a more powerful extract and embitters the drink.

She jams her staff into the earth by Ezra's skull. She says, "Drink this."

But the tanner is consumed by his pain, crying and groaning.

Naomi pinches his nostrils shut.

"Drink this. It'll ease the arthritis."

First the root, and then the leaves. And leaves will put him to sleep.

34

THE PAST: Ruth of Medeba
THE PRESENT: Ruth of Bethlehem

WHEN RUTH'S BLOOD RISES ON SOME STRONG EMOTION, her cheeks don't blush pink. They darken like a furnace in whose heart the deep fires glow.

She knows this. She's a Moabite, more swarthy than most of her kin and, to that same degree, less comely.

THE MOABITES ARE DESCENDANTS of Abraham's nephew Lot.

When the angels of the Lord came to Sodom and spent one night as guests in Lot's house; when they warned Lot and his wife and his two daughters to flee the city before God rained brimstone down; when he and his daughters settled in the hills above Zoar, the daughters feared that no man would be found to impregnate them. ("Our father is old, and there is not a man on earth to come into us.") So they served him wine until he was stupefied. Then they had sex with him. He never discovered the incest.

The firstborn daughter bore a son and named him Moab. When the Moabites migrated to the territory they now

215

possess, there were giants in the highlands, men of terrible girth and fierce antagonisms. They were called the *Emim*.

Israel encountered giants too, the first time they neared the Promised Land, just months after their flight from Egypt. Moses sent spies ahead to reconnoiter the terrain, the cities and their populations. The spies returned terrified: "We saw the *Anakim*, men so enormous we're like grasshoppers to them."

The people wept and complained and refused to go in and fight. Therefore the Lord punished the faithless. Israel wandered forty years in the wilderness, until that first, fearful generation had perished.

The Moabites, on the other hand, fought the Emim with courage and trust. By their cunning, with the power of Chemosh, their god, and under the command of a man named Chedorlaomer, they defeated the earth-shakers, destroyed them every one.

Ruth heard this tale while still a little girl—and learned as well the legend that attended it. For it was said, regarding the babies which the Emim could not deliver on account of the general slaughter, that their unborn spirits still moved among the Moabites. When the air grew thick with a stinking fog, an infant spirit would sneak into a sleeping Moabite—through her open mouth, on an inhalation. Once inside, the parasite would feed on the natural vigilance of its host, beclouding her eyes and numbing the flesh even to the stabs of a needle.

And these were the outward signs: the victim sank into a helpless lethargy, then fell into a sleep that could last a week or more. The longer the spirit's inhabitation, the worse the disease, for soft, tender swellings appeared on the back of the invalid's neck. If she didn't wake, her breath drifted quietly away, and she died.

Young Ruth was a scorched thing. Already at nine years she had developed big feet and a broad face and endurance and a determined self-control. Her hair defied a comb. For want of water she couldn't bathe, though she beat her poor clothing clean. These characteristics gave the girl two advantages. She became a trustworthy servant for the merchants who fed and rested in Medeba. They asked for her by name. And the second advantage: no foreigner considered raping her.

Ruth took small gifts — pinches of spice, scraps of cloth, bent pins, pretty thread, worn-out bridles — in exchange for watering and watching camels, or for preparing rich meals for the rich. She ate what they didn't.

In this manner Ruth supported her grandmother and herself, while saving something for marriage in the time to come. Well, she had no father. And, as far as Ruth knew, her mother had never married. Neighbors whispered that a Nubian goat had jumped the fence, but no one could prove the rumor, and her mother said that no better man had lived than the one who "fathered you, my daughter."

Then Ruth's mother died of that terrible sleeping disease.

Her grandmother had tried to draw the evil spirit from Ruth's mother by lying breast to breast on her. She put her mouth to her daughter's mouth. When the afflicted woman breathed out, the older woman breathed that same breath in, then breathed fresh breath into her daughter's bosom.

Ruth whispered, "What if the spirit comes out of her and goes into you?"

Her grandmother answered, "She will live."

"But what will happen to you, grandma?"

"It is a covenant of love. My last breath will be her first and her salvation."

Years later Naomi persuaded Ruth that it was not the unborn spirit of the Emim that had killed her mother, but the bite of an African tsetse fly.

Naomi, the Hakamah.

"Naomi, my mother."

SHORTLY AFTER DARK, Ruth returns to her mother-in-law, fairly burning with happiness.

Her robe bulges so heavily that the young woman carries the load by clasping her hands beneath it.

Close to the doorway Ruth kicks into something that grunts.

"Naomi! Did I hurt you?"

The pile produces an un-Naomi-like whine.

From inside the house Ruth hears the *chip-chip* of stone on flint. Sparks touch a wick then grow into a single lamp-flame.

"Naomi, there you are. Look."

Ruth kneels and, on the space between herself and her mother-in-law, pours out a mound of newly threshed grain. It raises a sweet, tingling dust. The women sit quietly, Naomi taking the measure of the gleanings, Ruth watching Naomi.

Naomi says, "An ephah."

"Not all my own doing," Ruth says. "The landlord told the reapers to let me glean among the sheaves. Mother, he told them to drop stalks with the ears still full."

Naomi repeats, "An ephah."

"He shared his lunch with me." Ruth opens the sling she'd brought home on her back. "Leftovers." She sets a bottle of sour wine on the ground and parched grain and dates.

"This one and that one spat on me. Envy, I think. But the landlord's sister came and kept me company. Her name is Basemath.... Please, Mother, eat a date. Drink some wine."

"Basemath," Naomi says. "What's her brother's name?"

"His sister called him Boaz."

Naomi sits absolutely still for several minutes, lamp-flame shadows wriggling in her face.

Then she says, "Blessed be he by the Lord, whose kindness has not forgotten the dead."

Ruth utters an earnest assent: "Blessed be he." And the heat mounts into her face once more.

Naomi says, "Boaz is kin to my husband Elimelech. Ruth, don't glean in any field but his."

The old woman takes a bit of parched grain and nibbles.

Through the next two weeks the younger woman gleans barley in the field of her kinsman Boaz ben-Salmon.

RUTH LIKED HER HUSBAND MAHLON. He was steadfast. Though he couldn't keep up with them because of his limp,

Mahlon worked doggedly beside his father and his brother. They carved household cisterns out of solid rock, or else they dug them in clay and plastered the walls water-tight.

Brother Chilion was a roisterer for races and play and hard work. Her husband proved to be the tender one. And a teacher. Ruth could speak four or five languages common to the traveling caravans. She knew that several of these could be painted on stone or leather or Egyptian reed-paper, or else pressed into clay; but she couldn't read the visible script. Mahlon could. The Israelites had learned it from the Canaanites. They applied it to their own Hebrew, and patient scribes passed the craft along.

Ruth was a quick study. Her husband wrote words in the dust, sounding them out. She imitated the drawings and the sounds—reading.

She liked Mahlon. But he would sob in the night, sometimes rising up crying, "The sword! The sword!" At other times he wept softly and would not be comforted. Ruth held him as though he were a child. In her strong arms she controlled his wild starts. She wiped his endless tears. She deciphered his mumbling sorrow enough to know he was grieving for a woman in his past.

There was no question but that Ruth would be a good wife so long as they both lived. She could accommodate and thereby be content. But Mahlon died, and who was left to her but Naomi?—whose determination and purpose the Moabite held in the highest esteem.

AND NOW THIS NEW THING COMES UPON HER and takes her breath away.

Boaz strides the barley field, and Ruth must struggle not to gaze at him. Nodding his brilliant turban to the laborers: "The Lord be with you."

And the laborers in genuine devotion: "The Lord bless you."

So too Ruth, in the silence of her mind: "O Lord, shower him with goodness and mercy." *Him*, because to say his name, even to think it, seems to break little dams within her, allowing a sweet aching to run free.

He walks beside that cricket of a foreman, discussing matters. He pauses, facing that portion of the field where Ruth is gleaning—looking at her!

O Ruth, keep your eyes down and your hands busy. Kill the expectations in you. Accommodate. The man has given you no sign. Yes, but look. Look there. Look at his blazing face, how dearly he is smiling!

The wheat harvest follows hard upon the barley harvest. The sun blares like a trumpet. Ruth wears widow's weeds, the black goat's hair that encloses the heat so that sweat pours down her spine. It pools below her throat and sticks beneath her breasts. She drinks water regularly. She still gleans the fields of Boaz. Wheat makes a finer flour than barley. It's important to fill their bins, Naomi's and hers, with a greater harvest of wheat. But she's a woman exhausted and disheveled with nothing to recommend to the male eye.

The landowner seems ever more distant now.

She is, after all, a Moabite. She speaks, she knows, with an accent.

At night in lamplight Ruth labors to write with a finger dipped in lampblack on a swatch of linen. In order to keep the letters from smudging, she covers them with another swatch of linen and folds the whole.

In the morning she tucks the cloth with parched grain in her shoulder sling.

Then at noonday she bites her lip and approaches Basemath.

"Please," Ruth whispers, fearful and hopeful at once. "Give this to Boaz."

The bright, healthy, loose-haired and long-legged woman puts the supplicant at ease. "Into his hands," she sings.

But the next day passes with no response.

And the next.

Ruth is ashamed of herself. Never, never, never has she acted so foolishly! Let the God of Naomi restrain her like a skittish mule—restrain her as surely as he has her mother-in-law. Be gloomy, Ruth! Remember your place.

On the third day, at the end of that day, she creeps again to Basemath.

"But your brother ... he hasn't ... I thought he would say something...."

"Oh, Ruth," Basemath smiles. "My brother can't read. But he *wants* to."

"Wants to?"

"To read what you wrote. So he's waiting to show it to a Levite. The Levite will—"

"Oh, no!" Ruth goes dizzy. "Not a Levite!"

Basemath looks concerned. "What's the matter?"

"I wrote ... I quoted ... Oh, Basemath, it's private."

"Priests keep secrets."

Ruth's private words: "His head is as the most fine gold, his locks are bushy and black as a raven. His eyes are the eyes of doves...."

"Oh, Basemath! Oh, go get the letter back before he reads it."

I am black, O daughters of Israel. Don't gaze on me because I am dark. It is the sun, not my soul. The sun has gazed on me and made me what I am.

THE PILE THAT LIES BY THE WALL of the house where Naomi and Ruth abide is human: Ezra, the tanner-that-was, now crippled stiff with arthritis and broken in his soul, lies crooked on a reed-woven pallet.

Naomi serves him as Ruth serves her. Old woman, older man, she spoons soup into his mouth. She squirts wine from the nipple of a wineskin. She brings a basin and rags, and lowers herself painfully, and washes the excrement from his stringy hams. Ezra is untroubled by the indignities. On the other hand, he squawks constantly, demanding that the women pick him up and carry him into the house, because "the ruttin' walls is mine, the ruttin' roof is mine, the ruttin' nooks is mine—and you ruttin' bitches robbed me out'n my rutting *house!*"

Naomi never answers. Since ministering unto him Naomi has seen no reason to address him at all.

35

THE PAST: Boaz Prepares Ground
for a Fig Tree
THE PRESENT: Abandons the Plan

FOUR MONTHS AGO, AS THE LATTER RAINS were coming to an end, Boaz told his sister it was time to remove the fig stump in their courtyard.

Basemath knew that for him the stump had been a lingering accusation because he himself had destroyed the living tree of his ancestors in a spiteful rage. Maybe, she thought, forgiveness had set him free. And if that was so, then her prayers for him were answered.

Basemath had taken cuttings from other figs and planted them in the vegetable garden Miriam kept outside the village. When one slip had matured into a small bush, Basemath asked her brother to come see it.

"Not the fig of our fathers," she said. "But who's to say it can't be the fig of your descendants, Boze?"

"I have no descendants," he said.

And Basemath said, "Hmm. Ponder that a while."

Boaz then sharpened his ax head, fixed it to a new poplar handle, and went to work.

The ancient roots underspread both the courtyard and the house. He laid his ax to a visible, burly root. At the same time he chopped a basin-like hole into the top of the stump. This he filled with dry mosses and on top of that, charcoal. He gathered willow sticks and bunched them around the stump, then set the whole on fire. He kept banking the coals inside the stump and around it, day and night maintaining a slow burn.

Boaz took to watching the smoky glow in the evenings. Basemath sat beside him, sometimes taking his hand. He permitted his sister's gestures of affection.

Boaz pried the flagstones up from the ground. He dug the rich old earth, shoveled it aside in piles, and went at the roots with strength and purpose.

No haste. Brother and sister were developing a new relationship. Basemath was fourteen. Soon she would have to leave him and his household. Marriage would change things forever. It was his, Boaz's, heart now quietly mourning —a smiling sort of sorrow. Basemath read through his dissembling.

Dig a little, chop some more. He dug a deep circular trench and cut through every root until Passover, after which the hollow stump itself was hauled out of the courtyard, out of the village and burned to ashes.

After Passover the barley harvest began. Suddenly all that had been well with Boaz seemed to harden into a stomachache. The corners of his mouth drew down.

Whenever she passed through the courtyard, Basemath looked at that ragged pit, and it saddened her. The flagstones still were stacked. The last rains had cut rivulets down the sides of the dirt pile. It was good ground ready for good growth. But Boaz had abandoned the task. He had turned away just when his heart had started to welcome his sister into the fullness of her womanhood.

Heart-sore, so it seemed, Boaz became an anomaly, one day bathing and trimming his beard to a fare-thee-well, the next going rumpled and unkempt to work. He wasn't eating. Basemath prepared his midday meals. She carried them out to the fields herself. Water, beer, a cool date wine, sage tea, milk: he scarcely sipped a thing. And he came home alarmingly fatigued.

She brought to him the linen Ruth had inscribed. She told him its source. He stared at it. Then he looked at his sister as if to ask, *Should I really take it?*

The tall, noble Boaz, son of Salmon, his spirit shrinking like the kernel in a walnut—he took the cloth gingerly, unfolded it on a shelf, and gazed at lines straight and curling, lampblack on a close-woven linen. He laid his big thumb under the writing. He leaned forward to sniff the overlarge handkerchief.

After the barley was harvested, threshed, winnowed and heaped on the threshing floor, Boaz now sends his laborers into the wheat fields: reapers, bundlers, gleaners.

The gleaners.

Setting food out for her brother at midday, Basemath follows the focus of his eyes. *That* gleaner! Ruth the Moabite. Ah.

In the afternoon she searches through her brother's tools and finds a bronze scoop the size of a man's hand, fashioned with a tang at the broad end. She tucks her tunic

RUTH

up around her thighs, and kneels in the courtyard, and starts to shovel the dirt back into the fig pit. The young woman works cheerfully, her raven curls covered with a scarf dyed yellow. Her cheer becomes her speed.

When Boaz returns from the field, he is met with a storm of flying dirt. Basemath smiles at him. He goes into the house. When the hole is a third full, she dribbles water over the soil.

Now she whets the leading edge of her scoop *(zip, zip,* in her brother's hearing) then takes the tool and a sackcloth bag to Miriam's garden. Evening is falling. Basemath cuts a wide circle in the earth around her fig bush. She digs down until she can ease the plant aside and flood its root-ball. The whole wet ball she wraps in the sackcloth, then drags the load back into the courtyard.

Boaz is waiting for her.

Wordlessly he helps his sister lug the bush into the hole prepared for it. Together they pack good earth around a new tree.

Basemath glances at the brother. *Oh, Bozy! How many important things we've accomplished today.*

With muddy clothing, dirty hands, fingernails black and broken, the two children of Salmon stop where they are and sit and look at the bush.

Basemath says, "I'm scared for you."

Boaz sits unmoving.

Basemath says, "You are brooding, Boze."

Boaz gets up and goes to the stair steps and climbs slowly to the roof.

The young woman loses cheer, loses all inclination to do anything but sit and wait for evening to pass into night.

But his tread descends the stairs again. Boaz sits down beside her, in his hand the finger-stopped boxwood flute. He begins to polish the instrument, using a cloth infused with bees' wax.

"Basemath," he says, then pauses. "If a man has the right," he strings the words together with an uncommon care, "to shape a woman's life according to his own designs ... I mean, if this is the way the world goes—" he stops polishing "—then I am undone."

She keeps her eyes on the fig bush. One day she will weave baskets from its leaves—when the leaves are long enough and the tree strong enough to sustain her little thefts.

Boaz says, "I can't get past the knowing. It's the knowing ties me up." Again he pauses. His jaw muscles clench. His clipped whiskers roll like animal fur. "Oh, Basemath," he says, "I know their minds, don't you see? I know how the women experience things. I know what they lose to a man's designs. I know ..."

He whispers this next in tones so much like confession that Basemath receives it as a kind of obligation.

"I know why young women walk the hills," Boaz says, "bewailing their virginity."

He moistens his lips and puffs air into each small hole in the flute.

"Boze?" she says. "Why are you so unhappy? How does this knowing—" No, she can't even figure how to ask the question.

They are equals. He treats her as his equal. But in this odd moment Boaz is behaving like her junior. Basemath has never met a man capable of laying authority aside and asking wisdom of a woman. Is it a weakness? Or wisdom? Does it come from his weariness? Or does it come from this terrible "knowing" of his?

She says, "You know the minds of women? This is what you're telling me?"

"Yes, I think I do."

He holds the flute up, inspects it, and peers along its length. The tube curves slightly—the natural way of the wood which he carved and sanded and bored.

Basemath says, "I don't understand. What's wrong with this knowledge?"

Her brother sets the flute down on the beeswax cloth. He turns and looks at her and holds the gaze through five beats of her heart.

He says, "This is the wrong. My knowing stops my mouth. Oh, my Balm, I can't talk with the Moabite anymore. A man with lands and power, don't you see? Ever since she shared my lunch that first day, I've become a man whose yearnings could hurt her. Lands and power! Heaven help me, how can I *not* but be the man who bends a widow and a foreigner to his own designs?"

36

"Today I'll Sew a Dress. Tomorrow I Will Hem It"

"Ruth," Naomi says sharply. "Come here."

Ruth is building a kiln outside the house, stacking bricks on bricks.

The harvest is in. The wheat has been threshed and winnowed, and waits in fresh heaps to be stored in the city granaries. Now that the gleaning is over and its benefits cut off, Ruth has sought some way to support herself and her mother-in-law.

Hence, a kiln in which to produce a better grade of fuel than sticks and dried manure. She plans to turn broom-tree roots into charcoal and to barter for their necessary supplies.

"Ruth, I want you in here," the voice a hissing of dry sand.

Ruth slaps dust from her hands and goes.

Naomi says, "Stand with your back to the wall."

Ruth does.

"No, straight! Stand straight, shoulders back, head-bone pressed against the wall."

Ruth does. She makes a rod of her spine.

Crabbed-faced, crabbed-fingered, Naomi shakes out a narrow bolt of cloth, supple, closely woven, and lets it hang to the floor. This is thread of the finest wool, the nap brushed to a high sheen: where did she ...? *When* could she have woven such stuff?

Naomi limps toward Ruth (hay-foot, straw-foot), her lips full of stickpins. She presses the top corners of the fabric on either side of the younger woman's chest.

"Help me." Naomi buzzes the command through tight lips. "Hold it where I put it."

Ruth pinches the corners.

"Higher."

Ruth raises the cloth to her clavicle.

Naomi measures the fall of cloth by the spread of her fingers, and marks her measurements with the copper pins. She says, "Today I'll sew a dress. Tomorrow I will hem it. On the third day at sunset, you will take off your mourning clothes, and wash, and yank that weedy hair straight, and oil your body, and put on the new dress, and go out into the night."

"But it hasn't been a year yet."

"I'll tell you where to go. I'll tell you what to do when you get there. Ruth, obey my words and maybe you'll get a living of your own."

"I don't want a living of my own."

"What you want means nothing." Naomi has finished measuring the cloth. She pulls it away and pins the top corners to the wall so that it hangs full length. "I'm old and tired and angry. If God hates me he'll kill me. If he loves me, he'll grant my wish and kill me." Her staff stands in its socket. Naomi grabs it and turns and looks hard at Ruth. "You can't live alone. The village will eat you up. We've got to persuade my kinsman to protect you."

O *Naomi, entreat me not to leave you.*

"Do what I say, step for step." This is turning into a speech, more words than the old widow-woman has uttered since the burial of Mahlon. Her tone refuses deviation. Her glare is a pair of iron nails. Once, years ago, Naomi sought a young woman's opinion regarding her future. Now she ignores another young woman's opinion altogether.

"Never mind the risk. Swallow pride. Forget fear. Move *through* the shame. Reach for security on the other side. Ruth! Obey me!"

37

A Woman Waiting in Her Courtyard, a Spirit Sailing Abroad

BETHLEHEM IS FAST ASLEEP. THE FIRMAMENT IS SANDY with the ancestor's stars. Somewhere a gutter-dog yaps. Another mongrel delivers itself of a couple woofs, but otherwise can't be bothered.

Reumah lies on her pallet beside a daughter. Her husband and their son lie crosswise in front of the door. Eglah occupies the upper room pregnant, beside a husband of her own.

The little boy coughs and turns over. Without waking, his father wraps an arm around him, encircling him with safety. Reumah sleeps on her back, hands flat on her abdomen, her chin thrust upward, popping her lips on every exhalation.

The Women of Bethlehem and their families plow sleep at various depths, some soils easy and friable, some hard as nightmare. Elderly sleepers grind and strain. Somebody whimpers. Now and again a sick man moans.

There is a watchman in the room above the gate, but not much watching is going on. The poor fellow has laid his arm on the windowsill and his head in the bend of his elbow. Watchman, watchman, dreaming of peace in the village. He won't notice the motion below.

Naomi is awake.

Long ago when her family was whole—especially on the day of Mahlon's wedding in Medeba—Naomi gave thanks to the Lord God because she expected grandchildren, God's promise of a future and of the continuation of her husband's name on earth. She looked for babies in her own arms. Surely Chilion would marry thereafter. But he was a second son, and at that moment Naomi had been given a reason to hope for the eldest of her eldest.

Again tonight the woman of disappointments prays. Prays? Rather she hectors the Almighty. Naomi has initiated a dangerous scheme. If the plan fails, Bethlehem will loathe the dark alien. Women will spit and call her whore. Men will leer, infuriating the women the more. Even just to imagine these slights makes Naomi's blood run hot. She lies alone in the little house. The wretched Women of Bethlehem! *Do not, God of the ancestors, give them the satisfaction.*

Miriam, the stepmother of Boaz, sleeps in peace, for he has elevated her life and the honor of her husband's name. Frail Rizpah will go to her grave lamented by many mourners. Her mother's body will not smell of corruption, but of orient spices.

Basemath is like Naomi. She cannot sleep. This young woman sits under the stars in the windless air of the courtyard, distressed. Her brother has not come back home. Nor could she find him earlier.

The laborers are in their houses. Late in the afternoon Boaz's foreman dropped by with his master's pouch and his pack, saying that he stumbled on them in the open field, and what if beasts would tear the leather apart? And was Basemath aware that Boaz hadn't celebrated the harvest home?

In fact, she feared as much. She spent the morning preparing a sumptuous meal with which to feast the success of his fields. At noon she took it to him—but couldn't find him. If he was among the jubilant crowds, he was hidden by them. He wasn't in the city gate, not on the terraces, not in the orchards, not under the trellised grapevines, not on the path that climbed the mountain.

It occurred to her that the farmer might still be working. She sought him on the threshing floor, where the grain was piled for the last task of the harvest. No, not there either. But she thought this the most likely place where he'd show up, so she waited. She swept the floor. She spread a leather sheet and set the meal here, placed beside that a cask of wine—enough to make a big man silly.

But by the evening she returned to the house. She lacked an appetite. She sits in the courtyard, yearning to jump up and *find* him, by God. But she sits and looks at the black shadow which is the young fig.

Under the powdery starlight, Bethlehem—its jumbled houses, the uneven surface of its many roofs, its crooked lanes—lies quiet and enclosed. Everything is common on this night in the month of Ab. Judah is not at war.

The heavier farming is done for a while. The sheep are in their stables. Midnight holds no surprises for hard-working peasants.

Beyond the city walls, pale hills emerge from the dark valleys.

But there is motion outside of Bethlehem's gate, a wraith passing by, having come from the southeast. A spirit of grace, soft in a dress sewn of a white feather-fall, sailing toward the farmers' barns and buildings.

The little dog must think itself the watchman, for it has been keeping pace with the ghost, she outside the wall, it rounding the inside, yapping, yapping.

38

"Spread Your Wing over Me"

MIDNIGHT'S STARS TOUCH THREE FORMS ON THE THRESHING floor. Two are rounded heaps of grain, between which lies the figure of a man, a shadow stretched out and the blacker shadow of the robe that covers him.

Ruth approaches tiptoe. The threshing floor is cool to her foot and well swept.

The Moabite is obeying her mother-in-law. At the same time she is compelled by her own emotions, though they whirl with contradictions. Ruth is like the untamed creature that cranes its neck toward food, while pedaling backward from the man that holds the food.

When he lies down, observe the place where he lies....

Boaz breathes a moist, gentle snore. A covered basket sits primly against one of the piles of grain. A casket lies within his arm's reach. It is wine that smiles in the man.

Then go, uncover ...

Ruth pulls a brooch from her dress. It parts all down its front. Her body is black between the dove-white wings of the cloth. A light breeze tightens the woman's skin.

237

Nevertheless, she slips her arms free one by one, and allows the supple cloth to fall and gather behind her heels. If wind were a washing, Ruth is clean, throat and breasts, pelvis and thighs.

Toward him, away from him, toward him—sweet body in the starlight.

Ruth kneels. She spreads her hands above the man's dark form, then slowly lowers them. His blanket is tucked up under his chin in the manner of babies and young boys.

Tenderness stirs her bosom.

She slides her rough palms under the edge of his robe and runs the tips of her fingers lightly down the man's warm flesh. There is the lumpish skin of a scar on his shoulder. He's wearing nothing but a loincloth—

The snoring stops. So does Ruth. An infinite minute passes. Then in a rush Boaz inhales a huge balloon of air and releases it in that gentle, dribbling snore.

Uncover, Naomi said. *And lie down....*

Ruth lifts the robe from the man's legs and deftly lies down beside him. She allows the robe to cover them both. She holds very still. Her heart hurts for pounding so fiercely. An anvil in her chest. She wants to pant. She is wild to pant. But she compresses her lips.

Suddenly Boaz shouts, "Holy God!"

He starts slapping at his legs.

Ruth takes a hit to her ribs. "Ow!"

The man throws off the robe. He grabs her hair. "A woman? You're a *woman?*"

Ruth shrieks. Her scalp burns. The night breaks into a fury of sparks.

Boaz sits up. "Who are you? What're you doing here?"

Ruth tries to answer. But her neck is bent too far backward. She tries to answer but makes a wailing sound.

Boaz lets go her hair. He clasps her ribs and lifts her into a sitting position.

"Who *are* you?"

She protects her face behind her wrists and whimpers, "Ruth."

He stops.

She doesn't know what's coming next. She hears his breathing and nothing else.

When he speaks it's with the clickings of a dry mouth. Boaz says, "You're naked."

"I'm *Ruth!*" she says.

"Yes. I know. You're Ruth — and you're naked."

What can he see? What shows in starlight? What ought to show? But Naomi has sent her here for a purpose. Purpose clothes her. Purpose emboldens her.

"Did I ..." Boaz swallows. "I didn't mean to ..." *hurt you.*

Ruth sits up straight. She places both palms on the floor. She expands her chest, her small breasts prominent, and goes one step beyond Naomi's commands. There is the mistress. There is the dignified.

Almost as an assertion Ruth says, "Spread your wing over me."

Boaz doesn't move.

"You chose to come," he says.

Ruth can feel his candid observation of her bare self, as though eyes in the dark can make indentations just by looking.

Stars creep across the black heavens, the cosmos study-
ing her. A chilly breeze picks up. Goosebumps rise on the
flesh of her arms. Her nipples harden.

Too much time. He's taking too much time. Ruth's bra-
vado weakens. The Moabite hunches her shoulders and
curves her spine till her forehead is pressed against her
kneecaps.

Oh, Naomi, what have I done?

In these slow, consecutive moments Ruth is becoming
the city's whore. And this noble man, this Boaz, whose
good will she hungers for with all her heart: how contemptible she must seem before him.

Ruth is dying the death — and the best she can hope
for is the landowner's forbearance, that he keep her sin a
secret.

Into the black pool of the threshing floor, Ruth lets fall
the words: "Have mercy on me."

She hears motion, a rustling of fabrics heavy and light.
Her dress floats down upon her shoulders.

"Ruth." He is behind her, standing. His tone is tender.
He says, "Ruth."

She draws Naomi's dress closed.

Boaz comes around and sits facing her. He remains
silent a long, long time. Ruth peeps up. The moon sends a
little light from the east. Boaz is robed and gazing steadily
back at her. Quickly she drops her eyes again.

Boaz says, "There was some writing. You sent me some
writing."

It was foolish, foolish. I never should have done it.

Boaz says, "I can't read. How can I know the words you wrote?"

Ruth is under indictment, her sins tricked out before her. A naked body now, a naked longing then, and the terrible presumption ever to think that nobility would look on her with anything like affection.

"Ruth?"

She begins to shake her head. There is no deserving in her. She should turn to dust and be blown away.

"No, no," Boaz says. "I won't accept it. You can't say no to me."

He moves. She hears the slosh of liquid. She feels his slow approach, and then the crook of his finger underneath her chin. She wants to weep.

But he lifts her face. She can't open her eyes.

"Once before I gave you wine to drink," he says. "It seems you need it now again."

At her lips she feels the edge of—what? She looks. It's a metal cup filled with dark wine.

"Drink," he says. He tips the cup for her. She can't help but look at him.

She drinks, looking.

"Good, good. And has my maiden's tongue been loosed by the wine?"

She drinks the cup dry.

He touches the hem of his robe to the dribbles down her chin, and says, "What *were* those words? What did you write to me?"

Ruth's cheeks grow warm. Not because she's under

judgment. Rather, she hears the words in her mind and is as embarrassed as a little girl.

Boaz says, " 'His head is as the most fine gold.' Is that a part of it?"

Ruth gasps. The *very* words! She covers her mouth.

"And then," Boaz continues, low laughter bubbling in his voice: " 'His locks are bushy and black as a raven.' Was that about me? Were you telling me what you see?"

"You lied!" Ruth yaps like that little barky dog.

"I *what?*"

"You said you didn't read it."

"I said I couldn't read. Not the same thing."

"Well.... Well, but it's private."

Boaz can't hold back the laughter. But he keeps it to a chuckle.

"Now you're laughing at me."

"No, no," he splutters. "Laughing at myself, because I know the words, but I can't understand them."

"Understand what?"

"I know 'eyes,' and I know 'doves.' What I don't know is how my eyes can be the eyes of doves." He opens his eyes as wide as possible. They look like the round stupidity of pigeons. And Ruth's restraints all snap. She starts to laugh. It gives him permission and he laughs the louder.

A little more moonlight. The laughter runs its course. And then Boaz's countenance becomes that of a landowner and an elder in Bethlehem.

He says, " 'Spread my wing over you.' Do you know what an Israelite means when she says that to a man?"

"Yes." It is the thing Ruth spoke on her own. This is a request one step beyond Naomi's instructions.

Boaz says, "The Lord God bless you, daughter to Naomi, wife of Mahlon, the man who was the son of my father's cousin and my father's best friend. You have shown more loyalty now than you did when I first saw you in the field. By coming to me—by asking that I spread my wing over you—you've set in motion God's ritual by which the name of Elimelech, your father-in-law, shall continue on the earth. Ruth, I am Naomi's kin. I can redeem her from poverty, and *we*—you and I together—can redeem her from childlessness."

Having delivered himself of this formal speech, Boaz relaxes. He is a man sitting on a threshing floor in the small hours of the morning, gazing so openly at the woman, Ruth, that her heart grows full, and just to gaze back at him is enough. All the world can stop now. It is enough.

Boaz cocks his head to the side and interrupts her sweet satisfactions. "Say it, Ruth. I want to hear it from your own lips."

Say what? What is there left to say?

"Say the thing that saved you from demeaning yourself in front of me. 'She is no whore,' I will say to anyone who wants to know. 'She is courageous and faithful and noble, for the thing she did required tremendous trust. She might have died,' I will tell them. 'But she has come alive.' That, Ruth. Say that. Say what an Israelite means by 'wing' and 'over me.'"

The woman reaches for both of the man's hands. They

fold their fingers together. She says: "Boaz, son of Salmon, will you marry me?"

I come to my garden, my sister, my bride,
I gather my myrrh with my spice,
I eat my honeycomb with my honey,
I drink my wine with my milk.

39

At the Dawning of the Day

IT ISN'T AS IF THE STOUT, RED-FACED FARMER IS LAZY. He and his three boys tend their fields with a calculating diligence. In spite of the fact that his field is smaller than, say, Boaz's field, his produce is equal to that man's produce. For this farmer has shown more ingenuity than anyone else in Bethlehem.

He has gone abroad to find better tools and to learn better agricultural methods. Iron plow points cut the earth easier and more cleanly than bronze. Moreover, the grim fellow has hand-tooled a seed drill to his plow. He plants in rows rather than broadcasting the seed. He doesn't lose it to the birds, does not let it dry up on clay pathways or watch it spring up and turn yellow and die in shallow soil on immovable rock.

But the man is a lout. He shares neither tools nor knowledge. He went and got them for himself. Let others do the same. Until they do, they are his advantage.

He threatens with mattocks any woman or maiden fool enough to think she can glean in his field.

Once he hauled the widow of his younger brother

before the town elders, seeking to gain possession of the properties left to her. The elders were helpless before the law. Much as they despised this man's greed, they ruled in favor of his heartless suit.

He does not share payment or water or celebrations with reapers, bundlers, carters. They don't work for him. Rather, he lords it over his sons, forcing them to perform impossible tasks, and over his wife and his daughters. But he sets them an intense example. No one in the family can keep up with him.

Call this farmer So-and-So. Because he rejects fellowship with his tribe, the stout man goes nameless in Judah. He is driven to compete, to crush and to prevail. He is the antagonist of Bethlehem, the dog that gobbles up the goodness of his neighbors.

Naomi calls him Achan. Servants and day laborers call him the Brass Ass.

But Lord Brass Ass, he doesn't care.

NAOMI IS FURIOUS. "Did I *tell* you to talk about marriage?"

Ruth needn't say *No*.

"A mistress! Mistress was all! Mistress was enough!"

Even Ezra pushes himself a safe distance from the feral old woman.

"The man can take a mistress without complications. He would have set you up with a workable living. Nothing to bar that way, Ruth. But you said *Marriage!*"

Naomi shakes the staff, anger lending strength to her legs.

"And you persuaded him. He *wants* to marry you. Listen to me: to want to marry you in public—God thump that man and his nobility—is to lose the *right* to marry you! Don't you understand that? We have a kinsman *nearer to us* than Boaz!"

"But ..."

Ruth has poured into clay jars a third of the grain Boaz sent back with her. He told her to get home before she could be recognized. *No one should know that a woman came to my threshing floor.*

She arrived in the false dawn. As soon as she dumped the sack on the ground, Naomi limped out of the house and asked how things went. What did Boaz do? What did he say?

Ruth laughed. She caught up her mother's hand. "Oh, Naomi!" Ruth had never—think about that: never?—Ruth had *never* been so happy.

And the laughter was infectious. The old woman said, "My daughter!" And she said, "But tell me what happened!"

Ruth began the story, worked it slowly, lingered over every precious detail.

At the same time she put her hands to good use. She gathered handfuls of grain and poured them into the clay jar.

His reaction to her womanness was such jolly fun. And her nakedness almost discombobulated the man.

He hit her.

He hit you?

Well, he thought she was a snake or something. Brave men! They can do mortal battle, sword to sword and dagger to dagger with the enemy — but when you catch them sleeping with the cover under their chins, slip some creature against their legs, and they cry out, as scared as little boys.

"He didn't mean to hit me," Ruth said. "Said so himself. Mother Naomi —" Ruth burst into a peal of laughter. "I can hardly say this. It's so ... miraculous! We talked about babies! Having *babies!*" She grinned as wide as the Jordan River.

Ezra stirred. "What the hell?"

Naomi didn't immediately share Ruth's exuberance.

She said, "How did that come up? What made you talk about children?"

Well, when Ruth did all the things Naomi told her to do, when she had displayed the fruits she brought to offer the man, while she still sat completely naked, it suddenly seemed to her that only one thing could purify the offering and protect the nobleman from accusations of lewdness and preserve herself from shame. The idea came all in a flash, and in a flash she said it: "Spread your wing over me."

"You asked him ... Ruth, you asked him to make you his wife?"

"I did! I did!"

"What did he say?"

"Oh, Naomi, he said *Yes!*"

The older woman's face grew hard. She worked her mouth like a grasshopper. Her eyes rimmed with red. Then she exploded. She whacked her staff against the wall of the house.

Ruth jumped. Sleeplessness and swift, spiking emotions had drained her of strength and left her febrile.

Naomi growled like a she-lion, "Did I *tell* you to talk about marriage?"

Ruth whispers, "But ..."

Naomi is shaking and blowing spittle with her words. Neither did she sleep last night.

"That relative, that nearer kin," Naomi hisses, baring her teeth, "is the farmer they call the Brass Ass. Oh, Ruth! Oh, my daughter, you have *destroyed* your future and yourself! That Ass *ruins* people! Heartless, unholy son of a bitch. He'll marry you for one reason, to work you and whip you hard as a mule!"

Naomi sags, gripping her staff with two hands. She says, "I've seen it before. I have seen what cruel men do to women. Fathers beat their daughters. Warriors rape virgins. Husbands throw their wives to wolves. And this jackal, this kinsman, oh, Ruth, he has first rights to you. Not Boaz!"

Ruth's legs melt into the ground. Her sight is suffused in pink. She sinks down.

Ezra is saying, "Listen to me, listen to me, listen to *me*—I know how to make the bastard eat his dung. You gonna listen to *me* for once? I'll tell you how to ..."

Then darkness cloaks the exhausted Ruth.

40

The Morning

BETHLEHEM'S VINEYARDS FLOURISH ON TERRACES AMONG groves of fig trees. The vines have been trained up the trunks and out the branches until they reach like a lattice from tree to tree. The broad, overlapping leaves create a shady canopy where sometimes trysts are made by young men with young girls.

Shortly before the bunches of grapes grow fat and ready for the cutting, the vinedresser constructs of poles and cord a temporary, wobbly watchtower. Grapes are too valuable to trust to the goodness of human hearts. Likewise, the vineyards of Bethlehem are each surrounded with a fence. The fences are hedges of thorny bushes piled high and impassable. And the type of bush the vinedresser uses is nightshade, native to the Israelite countryside: a coarse, stiff-branched shrubby plant, its branches and leaves armed with reddish recurved spines.

On this morning in the month of Ab, the Women of Bethlehem gather at the gate, then troop out with their jars on their heads, on their way to the city's cistern. After this chore they'll carry baskets to their vegetable gardens and pick vetches and chickpeas.

Boys and girls lead sheep into the harvested fields to graze. And goats. Oxen.

Some of the men select tools for building watchtowers. Others go out to the winepress with carts carrying large jars and a different set of tools. Bethlehem's two presses are hewn in rock right close to the vineyards. Their hard, flat floors are cluttered with leaves and twigs and spiders and the scats of small animals. They need cleaning before the grapes are dumped and the women crush them underfoot. These men will inspect the channel down which the juice will flow—and will place the wine jars into their niches for receiving the juice. Afterward, the mouths of the jars will be sealed with clay, leaving a small hole in the neck so that the gases can escape. Funky fermentation, praise, praise the Lord—and wine to slake a city's thirst.

EZRA SAYS, "YOU GONNA TEND ME, WOMAN?"

Naomi is looking at Ruth and cursing herself. The child unconscious, her legs bent beneath her, the white dress soiled—Ruth is not disobedient or a gold digger. She is naive.

Ezra says, "Gonna nurse me? Wash my flanks? Cook porridge for my poor gums? I gotta *know*, you cripple-stick."

Naomi shifts her vision toward the noise. It's Ezra, struggling to sit up.

"What?"

"Nurse me, wash me, feed me, y'old biddy, and I'm gonna *tell* you how to beat his Lordship, the Brass Ass."

"What? Ezra! What're you talking about?"

"Lookee here! The woman stoops to talk at a beggar."

Naomi turns on her staff. "My daughter needs a drink of tea."

"Woman! I'm trying to be *nice!* I got a *bargain* to make. And you go turning your back on me?"

She sighs. "What then?"

"Trick that Ass with a field. Ask him, does he want a field for free? Say, on account of he's the nearest relative to Elimelech, he gets Elimelech's field. Brass Ass, I *know* he's gonna jump at it. *Hoo-eee!* Make him hungry, hungry. Then stick that servant-girl-you-want-ta-get-rid-of in his face. See what Jack Ass says *then*." Ezra's eyes are narrow with the cunning Naomi saw in the tanner long years ago.

"Ezra," she says. "What field?"

"*My* field. It's *my* field fair and square. But—if you swear to take care of old Ezra all his days, soak his poor old bones, I'll let you—it's me *letting* you, now!—let you make my field into bait for catching bastards."

41

Noonday

THE MEN AND THE WOMEN AND THE CHILDREN of Bethlehem climb the slopes toward the city. They've left their tools behind. They'll return after a rest and a meal. They *can* take the time these days because the present labor isn't as hurried as was the harvest.

Boaz stands in one of the rooms inside the gate, his beard oiled, the jaw line twinkling, his clothing a drapery finely white, his arms and his face darkened by a farmer's days in the sunlight.

He greets the people as they pass. It's an expansive company. Good fruit to come: early figs (which are the sweeter figs); wonderful clusters of grapes (how long since the Lord has been this bountiful?); pomegranates and olives before all the vineyards have been harvested.

They nod. Grimy faces grin. Boaz exchanges blessings with them.

There are already three elders sitting on stone benches in the gate. These are ancient men long past the strength in their arms. As other elders come near, Boaz asks them likewise to sit. He has a legal issue which will need their adjudication. They stay behind and sit.

There is one man who does not come home to rest. It is not in his nature to rest.

Cheerfully, Boaz has sent his sister Basemath and his foreman with a donkey to inform the Brass Ass that his cousin has discovered some property which he thinks might belong to him (old So-and-So). But as this is a legal matter, would the man bestride his, Boaz's, best donkey and come before the elders?

The stout, red-complected cousin arrives, but not on the donkey. He pegs it on his own legs up the road, never not self-sufficient.

Boaz bows. Boaz must bow nearly to his waist in order to embrace and kiss his cousin. With a flourish he begs the farmer to take a seat. The farmer remains standing.

The farmer says, "So, what's the deal?"

Boaz takes a flask from Naomi, whom he has asked to serve the men during their deliberations. "Something to drink, sir?"

"I got no time for the fumosity. Clouds me my brains. What's the deal?"

"Naomi, the wife of Elimelech"—Boaz gestures to the old woman with a genuine reverence—"has remembered that her husband owned a field when they left for Moab. It was never sold, though others have worked it."

Boaz is informing both his cousin and the elders of the facts. He is beginning to make a case, though his tone is friendly and generous and sounds nothing like a testimony.

"Hmm," says the Brass Ass. "A field. You going where I think you're going?"

Boaz says, "Please, sit down. No need to exert yourself in the heat of the day. And truly, cousin, I beg you to share a bowl of wine."

The cousin sits, though stiffly. This time it is Naomi who pours the wine and offers one bowl to the stout farmer, another to Boaz. Crude Sir So-and-So: he slurps noisily until the bowl is empty, then looks up.

Boaz says, "Yes, I am, cousin. I'm going the way you think I'm going. Naomi and I have a deal we think will please you." He sips a little wine. "Listen to this: if you wish it, Elimelech's property falls to you, because you are his nearest relative. If you don't wish, well, then the property falls to me."

"Which field? Which one?"

Boaz describes the place as well as the produce one might expect in a year.

"Okay. Yeah. I know it."

The man thrusts his bowl in Naomi's direction. His short forearms are thatched black and muscled, his face and hair leonine. His eyes, however, and the twitching of his bramble beard are suddenly hungry. Simple man, simple greed, no disguising his emotions.

"Ever since she returned to Bethlehem," Boaz says, seating himself across from his cousin and placing the wine bowl carefully beside the man, "the wife of Elimelech has been living in an inexcusable poverty. As a price for her land she asks no more than half the first year's produce, and then you own it free and clear."

"Half *my* work in the field?"

"After which, as long as you and your sons and your sons' sons live, it'll be the whole of your work in the field. That is a long time for a healthy, sturdy bloodline."

The cousin stands.

"Done!"

"Good." Boaz scans the elders. "But before they render judgment," he says, "there's one more clause to consider."

"What the hell?"

Boaz keeps his seat. He grooms his moustache with a thumb and forefinger.

The blunt fellow is impatient. "What clause? Get it *over* with!"

Boaz calls, "Basemath?"

The girl appears around a pillar, raven hair in folds down her back.

"Bozy?"

"Please take the donkey to Naomi's house. Bring our friend in the manner that suits her nobility."

Basemath—not as tall as her brother, but an alabaster tower over the cousin who is puffing his cheeks—goes out the gate and leads the donkey eastward.

"Wasting my time, you high and mighty. *Finish* the deal!"

"Right." Boaz follows his sister with his eyes, then speaks with a ritual gravity. "Before God," he says, "a man's name must not pass from the earth. And the Lord God, in his mercy, has granted Israel a way to preserve a man's name even if he dies and his sons die and there seems no one left to keep the line alive."

"Claptrap and fog," the farmer blusters. "Claptrap and

fog. We *made* a deal." He points a stubby finger at the fore-most elder. "You witnessed it. I'm done—"

"No. We are not done. Sit!" Boaz loops out a long arm, lays his hand on the cousin's shoulder, and forces him to sit. "The elders know the Levirate Law," he says. "They are waiting for you to make one more decision. You cannot have one without the other."

"One what? The other what?"

"Field *and* wife."

The foremost elder confirms the law. "Boaz ben-Salmon knows Torah. The statute he refers to exists for the sake of men like your kinsman Elimelech."

If she had the legs, Naomi would jump up and pace, she is so anxious. This is the moment. Ruth's future hangs in the balance.

Boaz quotes the law that Moses wrote: "If a man die and have no child, the brother of the dead man's wife shall take her as *his* wife. And it shall be that the firstborn which she bears shall succeed in the name of his brother, that his name be not put out of Israel."

"You're confusing me. It's the wine. The fumosity. You wanted to cloud my brains!"

The elder says, "Let me interpret. If there is no brother, the Levirate duty passes to the nearest kinsman. That's you, sir. And since Ruth is the wife of Elimelech's firstborn son—who has also died, and his brother with him—Ruth is the woman whom it has become your duty to marry."

The Brass Ass cuts his eyes left and right, looking for an ally in the gate. Boaz's hand hasn't released him. He rubs his nose vigorously with the back of his wrist. "Well," he says. "Well." He looks like an animal trapped. "So it's me? Me that's ordered to marry your black Moabite?"

Naomi can't contain herself. "Yes," she yells *(you killer of women's spirits).*

"Well, I don't *want* to. How about that?"

Now Boaz removes his grip from the cousin and stands. "Why would you refuse a fine plot and its perpetual produce?"

"A fine plot? Fine damage! So let's say the *Moabite* produces. So she bears a son. So it's Elimelech's son—that what you told me? So who gets the fine plot *then*? Elimelech reaches from the grave and messes with *my* sons' living. No! No, no, no, no, *no!*"

We're there, Naomi thinks. *Almost, almost . . .*

"Calm yourself," Boaz says. "There is an alternative."

The Brass Ass is tarnished with gloom. "Yeah, sure. Go to hell."

"You'll want to hear this, cousin. I am Elimelech's kinsman too, one remove from you. Don't you remember I said, if you didn't wish the deal, it falls to me?"

"God helps them that help themselves," growls the farmer.

"You have the right. It is your *right* to say no. If you don't like the entanglements, I am willing to take your place."

"It's a trick. You're out to get me."

"No, I'm offering you liberation."

"Everyone's jealous. I'm modern. I'm smart."

Naomi shakes her staff. "You think it's a trick? You hate my Moabite!"

Boaz's cousin barks, "Take it! Take her. Take the field. Take it all."

Boaz says, "This is your decision?"

"What'd I just say?"

"It's witnessed, cousin. It's done."

"Yes, yes, yes, yes." He turns and starts to stomp away.

Suddenly a hacking laughter coughs and cackles and sullies the sunburned air.

"Hee hee, Farmer Fart. We *got* your ass! Hee hee. Hoo hoo hoo!"

Here comes Ezra, the tanner-that-was, crouched like a toad on the back of the donkey led by a grinning Basemath.

The Brass Ass shouts over his shoulder, "I'm done with the lot of you. Forever!"

"Hee hee hee! Jack Ass!"

"Ezra!" Boaz commands.

And then Ruth appears. Ruth of elegance and pliable quietness, wearing a dress washed white again, her head shawled. The Moabite's dark complexion glows with fires banked deep beneath her comeliness.

At her coming the gate is suddenly silent with wonder.

And Boaz stares. The tall man, silly with smiling, is undone.

Where another bride would cast her eyes to the side and down, Ruth looks straight back at Boaz.

"Wheee-oo," Ezra exults, "that high black is beautiful."

Naomi leans forward. "Boaz!"

Boaz comes to himself. He moves. Ruth likewise moves. He stretches out two hands. One of hers clasps the hemmed edges of her dress. She offers the other. He takes it in both of his, and stands still.

Sing, Naomi. Sing, O Hakamah. How can such an occasion be memorialized except by the song to sing it home?

> *Awake, O north wind! South wind, come,*
>   *And whirl across my garden.*
> *Breathe my fragrance far abroad,*
>   *A savor for my lover.*
>   *Bring hither, winds, my lover.*
> *I'll come into the garden, my bride,*
>   *And eat blackberry honey.*
> *I'll gather myrrh and every spice,*
>   *When all the winds are ready*
>   *And all your portals open.*
> *You are precious in my sight,*
> *(You are precious in my sight)*
> *And honored, (and honored)*
>   *And I love you....*

Part Four

THE HAKAMAH

42

THE FUTURE:

Giving the Story Away

IN THOSE DAYS THERE WAS NO KING IN ISRAEL. All the people did what was right in their own eyes. And a certain Levite, residing in the remote parts of the hill country of Ephraim, took to himself a second wife from Bethlehem in Judah.

It has been recorded, what Naomi knew by heart. The Hakamah had lived the story. In her last days she also told the story—which until then had stuck in her soul like a recurved thorn. Milcah. Her poor daughter's murderous rape. The raving destructions of Israel and Benjamin.

Only the marriage of Ruth and Boaz could finally draw the thorn and heal her soul and tune her harp and set her singing voice free to give the story away.

She never sang the tale in joy. Of course not. It was a horror through and through. But it was also the history of her people. The histories of the covenants which God established with the Children of Israel shall not be abridged. Without the story whole, it would become a self-serving legend. Both the people and the God who chose them would be distorted, cowled in a consoling lie. And the present generation, therefore, would always be baffled, would grow angry or frightened, because their torn bits of story could no longer embrace and name their real, full, unhappy experiences.

Then what? Then legends will be dismissed. False histories become contemptible in the eyes of the enlightened. God himself, the true God, will be shunned or despised or considered to be ancient, empty ritual.

And then what? God will be lost. People will think that love is all—a kindly, grandfatherly love. They will build their idols along the lines of niceness. Mercy, compassion. Not death. Not the requirements of covenants. Not the divine judgments of evil behaviors.

This love is more than the sweet desires of human imaginations. This love comprehends the whole of human experience and can name it all.

Naomi, Bethlehem's clear-eyed Hakamah, knew that without the hard histories, the days would come again when there would be no King of heaven and earth, and all the people would do what was right in their own eyes.

Nevertheless, it was hope that opened her throat and allowed the truth to flow forth: how dear was her daughter Milcah, Milcah of the white hands; and how terrible the loss of her. How surprising and divine was the gift of a second daughter, Ruth, the swart Moabite and the wife of Elimelech's kinsman, Boaz.

When the elders in the gate had witnessed Ruth's betrothal to Boaz, in one voice they said, "May the Lord make the woman who is coming into your house like Rachel and Leah, who together built up the house of Israel.

May you produce children in Ephratha and bestow a name in Bethlehem. And through the children that the Lord will give you by this young woman, may your house be like the house of Perez, whom Tamar bore to Judah."

Old, dry-stick Naomi raised her wrinkled face and blubbered for such a prophecy.

> *You have ravished my heart, O sister, my bride.*
> *You have ravished my heart with one glance of your*
>   *eyes.*
> *How sweet is your love, O sister, my bride.*
> *And sweeter your loving than spices and wine.*
> *My lover is mine and I am his;*
>   *He pastures his flock among the lilies.*
> *He brings me to the feasting house,*
>   *And his banner over me is love.*

They roasted the goat that Ruth and Naomi had led across the Jordan. Bethlehem danced at the wedding feast.

43

"Come to Me and Welcome Our Son"

BOAZ IS A WRECK.

He's pacing on the roof of a room newly built and attached to the side of his father's and his ancestor's house. He's brought wine and beer in jars and casks, and stacked the stuff everywhere. But he doesn't touch it. If he did, he thinks, he'll throw up.

No turban. His hair stands as erect as reeds on his head. Looks like a cow has spent the morning licking it. The tall man's beard is ragged. There are at least six other men keeping him company. But Boaz couldn't name them. He stares right through them. His spirit is occupied with anguish.

A mighty bellow arises from the house below.

The Women of Bethlehem, squatting in the courtyard and outside the courtyard and on the roofs close by, clap their hands and sweeten the air with ululations.

Maacah says, "She's got good hips, that one. I bet she shoots the baby out like a stone from a sling."

"*Yee-yaaaaaah!*"

Reumah grins. "That girl's a she-lion."

Another woman says, "You hear Naomi laughing? I think I hear Naomi laughing."

Boaz isn't laughing. Women's ways unman him. He has no desire to see the birth. But when Ruth yells, he wants to find a club and beat the enemy to death. What enemy? He scratches his scalp.

He says, "I should go choose a lamb. A yearling for Passover. Where are the shepherds? I'll need to talk with the shepherds."

A mumbling chorus of men's voices doesn't disagree.

"Yes, sir," says Boaz. "I'll go right now."

He slumps to sitting on the fresh carpet he bought the day Ruth announced her pregnancy.

Another tremendous howl below, and Boaz leaps to his feet, and the women answer Ruth's grand labor with ululation, and Boaz shouts, "What're we going to name him?"

"Him, Boaz?" one man says. "God told you it's a son?"

"Herzon? Name him Herzon? Or Ram? Amminadab? Nahshon?"

"There's no rush, brother. Wait'll he's a month—"

"My father's father's father's names. Five generations."

"Boaz! Sit."

In three strides he spans the room wall to wall, and three strides back again, and three strides ...

"Want some beer?" he says. "Anyone want to wet his gizzard with a swallow of beer?—ha ha." It's a cheerless laughter. "It'll calm your nerves," he says.

This is a Boaz transfigured. He *was* articulate, rational,

competent, graceful, gracious, affectionate ... noble! This man is a wreck.

A roar swells below, an ox-roar so tremendous it seems to heave the house.

Ruth, a woman of power, is delivering a son in Judah: *Hoooooooooooo-eee-yow!*

The world stops. Birds cease. Women wait. Boaz is fixed in a fatal silence.

Then his sister yells up from the courtyard, "Boaz? Bozy?" His Balm, his beautiful sister, Basemath. "Brother, come out!"

As if he were a lamb led, Boaz creeps out onto the open roof.

Basemath skips into view. "Boaz, you're a papa. It's a boy!"

Immediately the Women of Bethlehem exalt the Lord who does not forget the widow, the barren or the bitter. They rush upstairs to their own rooftops, and shake four hundred timbrels and thump the stretched leather. They pluck harp strings and spin and dance. The wind billows in their robes. Bethlehem becomes a garden, every woman a blossom, singing and singing blessings on their sister Naomi.

Boaz is overwhelmed. He believes that choirs of angels are circling the city.

Turning east, he falls on his face and calls on the name of the Lord:

"You have chastened me. I suffered the scorching sun and the lonely wilderness for my sins, O Lord. But now you've sent an angel, who says, *Deliver him from the Pit.* I have prayed to you, my God, and you have accepted me, and my life sees light."

Boaz, prostrate, prays, while daughters and grandmothers, wives and sisters chant for Naomi her last beatitude:

> *Blessed be the Lord, Naomi,*
> *Who has granted you a redeemer,*
> *Life again and nourishment in your old age.*
> *For your daughter-in-law, who loves you,*
> *Has borne him and laid him*
> *In your bosom.*
> *A son has been born to Naomi!*

In her heart, Naomi does not deny the blessing. She will praise the God of Israel again. But in her own good time. *She* will choose the moment in which to grant the Lord the favor of her return. But, well—soon.

BASEMATH BURIES THE INFANT'S PLACENTA—*"come out, little sister"*—in the fresh dirt piled around the fig bush in the courtyard.

And in that same day Ruth breaks tradition. She asks for Boaz. Would he come to her and welcome their son?

Boaz enters the birthing room with his hands crossed upon his breast. This is sacred. The smells in here are lusty and holy. His dark wife lies on a double-woven pallet, smiling with accomplishment. Oh, look and see: she is Lady Wisdom, by whom kings reign, whose fruit is better than gold, much fine gold, and who was there when the Creator made firm the circle of the sky.

Ruth says, "Look at our baby, Boaz."

Well yes. It's a baby, all right. A squash-headed baby, sleeping in the crook of its mother's arm, sucking on nothing except its gums.

She says, "Isn't he beautiful?"

Boaz squats down. He works his littlest finger into the baby's fist. The fist opens and closes on the big man's finger.

Actually, Boaz isn't sure what beauty Ruth is talking about. What he sees is long skull-bone and sweat-pips on a forehead as red as hard work. Threads of veins scrawl in the infant's closed eyelids.

But this, he thinks: this, now—his heir taking his finger in a mighty grip—this is beautiful.

"Ruth, what should I name the boy?"

Ruth says, "Kiss me, Boaz."

"Between Moses and us ... No, between Judah and us there are too, too many names."

"It doesn't matter," Ruth says. "Kiss me."

"The boy must have a name for the Book of Life. Remember Elimelech—"

Ruth reaches up and takes hold of his jaw and with reserves of strength pulls her husband's shock-bearded face close to hers, and kisses him.

His brain melts into merciful ignorance.

Ruth says, "Boaz, the baby *has* a name. It wasn't your job. The Women of Bethlehem gave your son his name."

"Oh."

"They named him Obed."

"Oh."

44

In the Fourth Generation after Naomi and Elimelech, a King Unites the Children of Israel

AFTER NAOMI'S HARP-STRINGS SNAPPED, AND HER PITCHER had broken at the fountain, and her breath returned to God who gave it to her in the beginning, the story passed to younger lips.

Ruth, the Moabite, became a Hakamah in Bethlehem.

She told the story to her son, Obed, and then to her grandson, Jesse.

And because God granted her to live in strength for three generations, Ruth, her eyes failing and her life-force dissipating, told the story also to her great-grandson, David, the son of Jesse.

Years after his great-grandmother had perished, David recalled her heritage. When his parents were threatened with danger and death, he sent them to Moab, where they lived in safety until their return to Judah.

But before that, David was a shepherd.

And the prophet came to his house and asked for him,

and he came in from the fields. He was a ruddy young fellow with beautiful eyes, as handsome as his great-grandfather Boaz.

The prophet took a horn of oil and anointed David in the presence of his brothers, and the spirit of the Lord came mightily upon David from that time forward.

And finally there was a king in Israel.